THUG

PASSION

4

(THE

FINALE)

WRITTEN BY:

MZ.LADY P

Published by Shan Presents

www.shanpresents.com

Acknowledgements

I can't believe I've made it this far in such a short time. This is my seventh book that I've written and I'm so astonished at my growth. I'm so grateful for all of my success.

I have to thank God first and foremost for all of his blessings. I ask that he continues to keep me covered in the blood.

My handsome sons Larry and Latrell inspire me to be the very best that I can be. Everything that I do is for them. My dream is to give you guys a better life and a better future. The sky is the limit for us. I love the both of you beyond measure.

My Mother Cornelia and my Father Moses raised me to follow my dreams and believe in myself. I've done just that. I love the both of you with all my heart and soul.

I would like to thank my siblings for their continue support. Your opinions mean the world to me.

I have to give a very special shot out to Tatiana Vaughn(Sister), Micha Vaughn(Sister), Talisa Willis (Cousin) and last but not least Ramona Williams(Cousin) Thank you ladies so much for listening to my ideas and my plots. Y'all listened to me until I got it together. Thank you guys so much for your love and support. Not only are we related, but you guys believe in me and support me wholeheartedly. Never been fake to me and for that I love you ladies from the bottom of my heart.

I would like to thank my Publisher Shantoinette Richardson for all of her hard work. I appreciate all that you do for me and the other authors at ladies at Shan Presents. #SalutetotheFirstLady

Team Bankroll is the Squad. I rep it to the fullest. Shot out to David Weaver he gives all of us authors the motivation to werk harder.

He's a living testimony that if you dream big you'll live big. #SalutetotheBawss #TBRS

To all my ladies at Shan Presents the best is yet to come for us. Let's keep bringing that heat for our readers. I'm so proud of each and every one of you. It's an honor to be a part of such a great movement. #TeamShanPresents

I would like to dedicate this book to my Readers without you guys I'm nothing. Thank you for all of your continued support!!!!!

TEXT SHAN TO 22828
TO STAY UP TO DATE
WITH NEW RELEASES
SNEAK PEEKS AND
MORE....

Chapter One- Thug

Fuck My Life

As I was put into the back of the squad car, I watched as they also placed Tahari inside of the squad car that was next to me. We both just stared at each other through the glass. Tears were streaming from her eyes and I knew why. I couldn't worry about that right now. I had bigger shit on my plate to deal with.

I watched as Sarge, Malik, and Dro pulled up and jumped out the car. The police immediately held them back from crossing the yellow tape. It hurt my heart as I observed my mother crying and hovering all over the nigga Quaadir as they put him in the back of the ambulance. I laid my head back and shed a tear.

Not because I was going to jail, but because the two people I trusted with my life had been fucking with the enemy. Shit would never be the same after this.

I had been sitting in the interrogation room for over six hours and I was ready to take my ass to County.

"I hope you know. I have every intention on putting your ass away for the rest of your life!" The detective said as he slammed my head into the table.

I swear they had been working my ass over since they got me in this room. The shit was funny as hell to me. I had this shit in the bag. I had been asking for my lawyer since I came into the room and they continued to question me. The fucked up thing about this was that they weren't really questioning me about me shooting that bitch ass nigga Quaadir. I was getting my ass whooped over Detective Grimes and Nico.

I had offed them niggas so long ago I forgot about their asses. The detective that was interrogating me was Detective Grimes' partner. That told me this nigga was gunning for me. Unfortunately for his bitch ass, he just signed his own Death Certificate.

"Your wife had already told us that you and your crew killed them. Now, where the fuck are the bodies at?" At this time, he hit me so hard, I swear I felt my nose shift. I shook that shit off like the goon I was. I wished I wasn't handcuffed I would beat his motherfucking ass.

"My nigga you're going to have to do better than saying my wife told y'all bitch ass anything." I laughed at his ass and spit blood on the floor. The door swung open and my lawyer and the police Sergeant came into the room.

"Why is my client bleeding and why is he handcuffed to a table? I see a lawsuit against the Chicago Police Department. I strongly advise you to take off those cuffs." My lawyer Bill Gates played no fucking games. I'd paid a lot of money to retain him. This nigga was a beast in the courtroom. He had never lost a case and always came through for my team and me. I was about to enjoy watching him work.

"Detective Jones, in my fucking office now!" the Sergeant yelled to the detective that I was previously alone in the room with. "Mr. Kenneth, I'm so sorry for all of this. Please let me know what we can do about this situation." They left the room and I was now alone with my lawyer.

"Have you talked to Tahari yet?"

"Yeah. She was just released. She told me to tell you she would be at court in the morning. You go before a judge in the morning for a bond hearing. I'm pretty sure you'll get a bond. Especially since the guy you shot had two guns in his hands when the police arrived on the scene." That shit was music to my ears because I definitely was not in the mood to be sitting in the County Jail behind this bitch ass nigga Quaadir.

"Did I off that nigga?"

"I talked to Peaches and he made it out of surgery." The sound of my mother's name made me sick to my stomach. I couldn't believe she was at the hospital with this nigga. I didn't give a fuck if that was her son or not. She never gave a fuck that I was carried out in handcuffs. Peaches and I had always been close. She totally disregarded me as her son. I didn't care how old you were or how much of a gangster a nigga was, his mother's love was everything to him. For Peaches to say fuck me; had me hurting like a little ass boy.

"Going forward don't discuss my case with my mother or my wife."

Bill looked at me like I was crazy, but he knew not to speak on it. I knew it seemed as if I was acting like a bitch, but I didn't give a fuck. My family was everything to me and it was going to be a minute before I got over their disloyalty.

After discussing my case for about another hour, I was led to my cell. I laid on the bunk and all that I could think about was Tahari and my kids. I loved my wife with all of my heart, but I was not sure if I could get over her fucking my long, lost twin brother. She could deny it all she wanted, but I was not a motherfucking fool. I know she gave that nigga my pussy.

Chapter Two-Tahari
The Truth Shall Set You Free

I was happy as hell when they released me. I was nervous
because they kept asking me questions about Nico and Detective
Grimes. They had me fucked up if they thought that I would ever
snitch on myself or my husband. I lawyered up on their ass and they
left me alone. I was crying my eyes out because I could hear them
through the wall beating Thug. They did that shit on purpose
thinking that it would break me and make me tell some shit. My
husband was a gangster. Them bitch ass punches they were handing
out wasn't shit to Thug. I heard him laughing at their ass and I was
on the other side of the wall laughing as well.

I was still in shock and awe at how everything unfolded. I
couldn't believe that Quaadir was actually Thug's brother. I felt sick
to my stomach knowing that I had sex with him. That shit was just
nasty. I was glad I lied and told Thug that I didn't have sex with him.

Now that I thought about it, Quaadir told on my ass talking all that shit.

I could only hope and pray that everything Thug and I talked about prior to the shooting would help me out. My husband was not a fool though. He knew something happened between us. I saw it in his eyes as he sat in the back of the squad car. He wouldn't even look at me.

Thug was really hurt by Momma Peaches and her actions. I couldn't wait until they released my baby. I knew that he needed me more than anything right now. There was still so many unanswered questions. I'd been wrecking my brain trying to figure out what would drive Quaadir to come after his own family.

I couldn't wait to get home to my babies. I hadn't seen them since the night I was arrested for shooting Thug and that bitch Yoshi. I hauled ass running into the house when the cab pulled up. Marta was in the kitchen sitting at the table while sipping on some tea. The house was quiet so I knew that the kids were sleeping.

"Hey, Marta. What are you doing up?" I asked her as I grabbed a bottle of water from the fridge. I went back over and joined her at the table.

"I'm up worried about you and Mr. Kenneth, but I'm really worried about your children. Please forgive me, Mrs. Kenneth, if I'm over stepping my boundaries, but y'all are fucking up as parents." I was taken aback by her choice of words. Marta never spoke out of term ever. So, I knew she was really upset with us.

"I'm not sure I understand what you're saying."

"Everything that you and Mr. Kenneth go through affects those kids greatly. Ka'Jaire Jr. and Ka'Jairea are not babies anymore. They know what's going on. They have cried every night since you've been gone. I know that you love Mr. Kenneth, but you have to start putting those kids first. They all have been through so much. Kaine was supposed to get his cast off last week. I couldn't take him because I'm not the guardian, Mr. Kenneth was not available, and of course you were in jail."

I put my head down in shame and I started to cry. There is definitely something wrong when your Housekeeper/Nanny had to call you out on your parenting skills.

"I think it would be best if I took a vacation. I need a break from raising your kids. I make everything so easy for you guys. Please don't take this as a sign of disrespect. I love all of you like my own family and I know that you guys love me. This is for your own good." Marta got up and kissed me on the forehead and walked out of the kitchen.

Not long after, I wrote her a check for ten thousand dollars. She deserved a nice vacation for all that she had done for us. I assured her that there were no hard feelings for her expressing herself. Actually, I agreed with what she said. This street life and infidelity was getting the best of us. Thug and I needed to do better by our kids.

***

The next morning was hell getting the kids all dressed and off to court. I just knew we were going to be late. We all made it just in time. They called his name as we found our seats. The rest of the family was already there minus Peaches. Tears came to my eyes as I watched them bring him out in cuffs.

"Daddy! Daddy!" The kids all started calling and reaching out for him. Ka'Jaiyah went crazy because she couldn't get to him. That upset the babies, so I was escorted out of the courtroom. I had never been so fucking embarrassed in my life. Moments later Malik, Dro, and Sarge came out of the courtroom.

"What happened?" I asked because I was so anxious and ready for Thug to come home. I felt responsible for everything.

"They set his bond at twenty thousand. He has to fight the case though. We're on our way downstairs to pay it," Dro said as he hugged me and played with all the kids.

"Take the kids home, Lil Sis. We'll all be over there as soon as he is released," Malik said and they all headed downstairs to pay his bail. I headed straight home so that I could cook dinner and get the kids situated.

Once I made it home, I started cooking. I decided on Shrimp and Chicken Alfredo along with Garlic Bread. It was a process when a person got bailed out, so I knew it would be a while before Thug made it home. Time seemed to pass by rapidly. The more time passed the more I became worried. I started calling everyone's phone, but no one was answering.

Since I couldn't get in touch with the family, I decided to call the jail. I found out that he had been released hours ago. I hoped and prayed that he was okay. His phone must have been dead because it was going straight to voicemail. What started out as hours ended up as days. Thug didn't come home and my heart was so hurt. Not even a phone call or a text. The walls of my house were starting to close in on me. I knew that the kids were tired of the house, so I decided to take them to meet Cassie. I hadn't seen her since the night I went to jail. I needed someone to talk to outside of the family.

****

"They're so beautiful, Tahari. What are their names?" Cassie kissed and hugged each one of the kids.

"Ka'Jaire Jr., Ka'Jairea, Kaine, Kash, Ka'jaiyah, Kaia, and Kahari."

"Yeah, you definitely love your husband." We both shared a laugh. The thought of Thug brought tears to my eyes. I couldn't believe I still hadn't heard from him.

"What's wrong, Tahari?" Cassie moved closer to me on the couch. Although we were trying to build our relationship up, I wasn't quite ready to divulge all of our personal business to her.

"Nothing. I'm okay." I looked down at my phone to make sure I hadn't missed a call or text.

"Is everything okay with you and Thug." Cassie moved my hair from my face. At this point, she could see that I was crying. I hurried up and wiped my tears away. I hated to appear so weak in front of her.

"To be honest, I don't think he loves me anymore."

"Let me tell you something, Tahari, that man loves you. I can tell by the way he goes so hard for you. Thug worships the ground you walk on. Just give him some time. I promise he will come around. He's been through a lot lately." Cassie got up and started playing with the kids and all I could do was think about how much I had been through as well. My phone went off alerting me that I had a text. I looked and a smile spread across my face because it was from Thug.

Thug: Where are you with my kids?

Me: I took them to the park and to meet Cassie. Where the fuck have you been?

Thug: Bring my kids home right now!!!

I wasn't really feeling his texts. I chose not to text him back and just go straight home.

"I have to get home and cook for the kids. I'll call you when we make it home." I kissed Cassie on the jaw, gathered up my babies, and we left.

The whole ride home I was nervous as fuck. I was mad and scared at the same time. I had no idea what type of mood Thug was in. As soon as we entered the house, he was sitting in the living room. There was a fifth of Remy and rolled up blunts on the coffee table. He was definitely mad. Thug never drank or smoked that way in front of the kids. He knows that I hated for him to even drink in the living room.

"I missed you so much, Daddy!" Ka'Jairea ran into her daddy's arm. Ka'Jaiyah made sure to push her way right through all the other kids to get to him. The other kids didn't stand a chance with her around. I stood there and smiled at how much they loved their Daddy

"What's up Daddy's babies? I missed y'all too." I watched as he kissed and hugged all of our children. He acted as if I wasn't even standing there. I just stood there biting my bottom lip. I was trying my best not to cry, but Thug was making it so hard. During our relationship there, had never been a time he couldn't keep his eyes off of me.

"Don't take them anywhere unless you run it by me first!" he said through gritted teeth, but in a low tone so that the kids didn't hear him. At this point, I became so livid. I couldn't go off on his ass in front of my kids, but this shit was not over. He had blew the shit out of me.

Since he was kicking it with the kids, I snatched one his blunts off the table and grabbed a bottle of Moet from the refrigerator. I needed to calm my nerves. I went straight to our bedroom. I slammed the door so fucking hard a picture of us fell off the wall. Not long after, he came in the room and went straight into the bathroom. He closed the door behind him. I couldn't take it anymore. We had to talk about this. I got up and opened the bathroom door without knocking. I pulled the shower curtain and I instantly became wet looking at his body. My mouth watered as I looked down at his dick. It took everything inside of me to not strip and hop in the shower with him. Fucking wouldn't change the thick tension going on between us, so it was better that we dealt with the bullshit now.

"Can I please take a shower in peace?" He had his face screwed all up.

"You can take your funky ass shower. I want to know what's going on. How could you just get released and not come home for days?"

"The same fucking way you got released and went to fuck that nigga!"The veins in his head and neck were sticking out. He pulled the shower curtain back closed.

"I didn't fuck him, Ka'Jaire!" I had opened the shower curtain back and I was trying my best to wrap my arms around him. I didn't care that I was getting wet. He was roughly pushing me and pulling away from me.

"Get the fuck of off me! Real Talk. If you know like I know, you'll get the fuck away from me." He said through gritted teeth as he held my wrists. He stepped out of the shower and grabbed a dry towel. He walked out of the bathroom and I just stood there crying and in shock.

We'd had heated arguments, but this was different. His eyes were so dark. He looked at me with hatred and disgust as he talked to me. I gathered up the courage to exit the bathroom. Thug was getting dressed to leave. I was too afraid to say anything to him. So, I climbed in bed and pulled my knees up to my chest. I hated that I was so weak at the moment.

Although Thug didn't hit me, his words were fucking me up mentally. I watched as his phone went off a couple of times and he kept pressing ignore. He never did that, so I knew it was a bitch. Something inside me had me feeling like he was still dealing with the bitch Yoshi. I watched as he started putting on some clothes. I couldn't believe he was getting ready to leave and he had just came home after being M.I.A for a fucking week.

"Where are you going, Ka'Jaire?"

"Out!!"

"Why are you being so disrespectful towards me? I'm not that bitch you trying rush out the door to. In case you forgot, I'm Tahari nigga. Your wife, your Bonnie, your ride or die bitch! If you're mad at me about this Quaadir situation let's address it."I had jumped off the bed and was standing directly in front of him staring him in his eyes. He pushed me up against the wall and stared into my eyes. His eyes were watery and I knew he was about to shed some tears. That made tears well up in my eyes.

"Did you fuck that nigga?" I thought real hard about the consequences behind me continuing the lie or telling the truth. At this point I did what I thought was the right thing to do. Tears streamed down my eyes rapidly.

"Yes. I'm so sorry Baby! Please forgive me." He hauled off and punched a hole in our bedroom wall. It caused me to jump and cower in front of him. He had me scared shitless.

"So, you lied to me, Ta-Baby? I asked your ass and you lied to me with a straight fucking face!"

"I was scared you were going to leave me." I had slid down the wall onto the floor. Thug was standing over me with his fists balled up.

"Don't start all that fucking crying now. Your ass wasn't crying when you was fucking that nigga. I swear to God I want to lay hands on your lying ass. I can't do this shit no more, Ta-Baby. The house is yours. You have access to all the money. I can't stay here or I might hurt your ass. I'll call you and we can work out a schedule for the kids to spend time with me." Thug tried to walk out the room, but I latched on to him like a child.

"Please don't leave me, Ka'Jaire! I'm sorry! I'm sorry! It was a mistake and I'm so sorry for it. I'll do anything, please don't leave me."

We had found our way into the hallway. I guess my crying and hollering woke up the kids. They were all now crying. Thug roughly pulled me off of him and went into each of the kids' room. I just laid there in the hallway on the floor crying. He stepped over me and kept walking.

"I'm sorry! I'm sorry!" I hollered and said those words to him until I heard the front door slam. I laid on the floor and continued to cry. I couldn't believe our marriage was probably over and I had no one to blame but myself. If I would have known things would've turned out this way I would have never told the truth.

Chapter Three- Peaches
Family Matters

I know that it might not seem like it, but my kids are my world. I had just made some poor decisions. All the secrets I kept from them were to protect them. But all it had done was hurt them and cause my family pain. It was crazy how life could be cool one minute and the next all fucked up. I had never meant for anyone to get hurt behind my actions. I had been calling Ka'Jaire all day and every day. He refused to answer his phone or respond to my texts. I wish he knew how he was hurting me. Ever since he was a little boy, we'd had a special little bond. We're more than mother and son- we are friends. We could tell each other anything. Now that I sit here and think about it, as close as we were, I should have told him about having a twin.

It had been a week since the shooting and Quaadir had yet to wake up. I hadn't left his side not for a minute. Malik, Ta'Jay, and Thug didn't understand why I was here and not with them. It was simple. I'd raised them since the day I gave birth to them. Quaadir had never even experienced a mother's love. I owed him this much.

Quaadir and I had only talked on the phone only once before we met up. The day I went over to his house was my first time meeting him in person. We immediately recognized each other as soon as he opened the door. I was shocked to know that I had been around him a couple of times before.

While Thug was in Miami, he was dealing with Tahari. He went into defense mode as soon as he saw me. He started saying I was setting him up for Thug. I told him that I was his mother and he started laughing like it was some big ass joke. Seconds later is when Thug and Tahari bussed in the door. I watched the way he looked at Tahari. The way he was talking I knew they had sex. That shit drove Thug crazy.

Thug was overcome with jealousy and that was what really caused him to shoot Quaadir. I didn't know that it was Quaadir behind all the bullshit that was going on. I still couldn't believe he was behind kidnapping my grandbaby and most likely behind Thug's shooting. There had to be a logical reason why he had been doing this to us. I think that was another reason why I hadn't left his side. I wanted to be the first person he saw when he woke up. I just had to know why he would try and bring harm to us.

"Who are you and why are you in here?" I had to turn all the way around in the chair that I was sitting in to see who the loud mouth bitch was that was questioning me.

"Excuse me. This is my son. Who the fuck are you?" I was now standing up and in this bitch face.

"I'm Keesha his wife. We've been married for years and I never heard of you. I suggest you get your ass out of my husband's room."

"I strongly advise you to pipe the fuck down. This ain't what you want. You have me fucked all the way up little girl. I will beat your ass like you stole something. So, let's try to this again. I'm his mother, Peaches. Now, whether you never met me or heard of me is neither here nor there. The question is where the fuck have you been at? He was shot over a week ago. A real wife would have been here on the first thing smoking. So, miss me with that I'm his wife shit."

"What the fuck is y'all doing all that yelling for?" We both turned around and Quaadir was trying to sit up in bed. We both rushed over to his bedside.

"Oh, my God! I'm so happy you're awake." Keesha raced over to him and kissed him all over his face.

"What the fuck are you doing here and where are my kids?" He roughly pushed her back and I saw that same mean streak in him that Thug had. They might be fraternal twins, but they have identical personalities.

"Calm down, Quaadir. Don't push her like that." Despite wanting to slap this bitch's teeth down her throat, no child of mine would be abusive to a woman in my presence without me addressing their behavior. I was a woman before I was anything. I grabbed some water and put it up to his mouth, but he pushed it away.

"What are you doing here?" Quaadir asked as he turned his face up in disgust at me.

"I'm your mother and I wasn't leaving until you woke up. I know that I'm probably the last person you want to see, but I'm just trying to get to know you. I need to get an understanding on all of this bullshit that's going on."

"It's too late. I'm twenty-eight years old. I always wondered what you looked like or what you smelled like. Now that I know who you are, you're even more beautiful than I imagined. This is a lot to take in right now. I wish that we could have met under different circumstances. I don't think we can ever come back from this. Leave me your number and I'll call you as soon as I can."

It hurt, but I had to respect his wishes. As I gathered my things to leave, I made it up in my mind that I was going to bring my family together. By any means necessary.

"Ms. Peaches, can I speak to you for a minute?" I had exited the room and Keesha had stopped me. She better not be on no bullshit because I was going to whoop that ass.

"What the fuck do you want?"

"I just wanted to say I'm sorry about earlier. It's just that I've been through so much in Atlanta. Quaadir just left me and our kids. When I came in, I just knew you were the other woman. It was never my intention to be disrespectful. Please forgive me." My motherly instincts pulled her into my embrace because obviously she needed a hug.

"If you don't mind me asking where are the kids now?"

"They're downstairs in the play area." The sound of Quaadir calling her name on the other side of the door caused her to jump and get ready to go back inside.

"Take my number down. I'm having a family dinner next week and I would love for you to come and bring the kids. I also would love for you to meet the rest of the family."

"Okay. I'll see what I can do." She took my number and went inside of the room. I could hear Quaadir chastising her as if she was a child. He was going to be harder to get to know than I thought. I hoped this family dinner brought us all together.

Chapter Four-Quaadir
Who is God?

The thought of knowing who my birth mother was had a nigga all fucked up. Growing up, I always wondered who she was and what she looked like. Now I know that the woman who had raised me as her own was Peaches' aunt. All my life I knew that she wasn't my mother. She told me that one day she would tell me who she was. Aunt Ruth had been everything to me; a mother, a father, a mentor, and my very best friend. I wanted for nothing growing up. That sweet old woman gave me the world and at the same time she taught me how to conquer it.

Growing up, Aunt Ruth exposed me to the drug game. She was one of the biggest heroin suppliers Atlanta had ever seen back in her day. She taught me everything there was to know about the drug trade and how to get money. I'd been running the empire since I turned eighteen years old. Here it was ten years later and I was still running shit like the motherfucking Boss that I was.

I reigned supreme in the A. When I first started slanging dope, I had this old head who was a fiend; he started calling me God because my heroin was the best shit he ever head. All the fiends started calling me God and the name stuck. The bitches loved me and the niggas hated me because they couldn't be me.

Despite being head of my own empire, I was also a contract killer and that was where my hard on for Thug came in at. It was never nothing personal because I didn't know the nigga. I was contracted by some of my associates from Chicago to off that nigga. I didn't ask no fucking questions. If I killed him, in return, I could set up shop in the Chi and take over his streets. This shit was business for me from the jump never personal.

I knew about their whole family before my plane landed in the Chi. It was through pictures that I saw Tahari for the first time. She was so fucking beautiful to me and even more beautiful in person. I had to have her, but she loved that nigga Thug even in death. I really hated that she was in the middle of the bullshit. She was a good, loyal female that deserved to be happy. She was the type of woman a nigga needed by his side in these streets. I watched how she held that nigga Thug down when they came to the crib. She looked sexy as fuck with her gun cocked and aimed. That shit straight turned a nigga on. That was until it was revealed that Thug was in fact my twin brother and that shit had me completely fucked up.

I never even knew I was a twin. The only thing Aunt Ruth told me was that my mother loved me, but was too young to care for me. I really wanted to talk to Peaches, but I was skeptical. There was still beef with this nigga Thug and his crew. I knew he had every intention on finishing me off. I hadn't heard from the bitch Kenyetta or the nigga Bolo. That had to mean their asses were dead. Kenyetta better be lucky they killed her ass first. The stupid bitch had kidnapped a fucking baby without my permission. Her ass was only good for one thing and that was my dick down her throat and half of the time she couldn't get that right.

I was shot three times in the chest. If I wasn't in so much pain, I would get the fuck out this hospital and back on the first thing smoking to the A. Knowing that these people were my long, lost family. I had no desire to bring anymore harm to them than I already have. Especially Tahari, I hated that we took it to the next step. I could only imagine what Thug was probably doing to her.

****

"You didn't hear me calling your motherfucking name!" I had been calling Keesha since she followed Peaches out of the room. There was nothing for them to talk about.

"I'm sorry, Quaadir. I was just apologizing to her for what I said to her earlier," Keesha said as she came over to my bedside and kissed me on the lips. Keesha and I had been together since we were fifteen years old. I loved my wife, but I loved the streets more. I had put her through a whole lot. It surprised me that she was still around after all this time.

"Didn't I tell you no matter what happens do not leave the motherfucking A?"

"Yes, but Aunt Ruth wasn't trying to hear that shit. She told me to pack up Naadia and Niveaa and come here. She said you would need us to be with you. I had no idea you were shot until I went by your house and one of the neighbors told me."

"You can book a flight and take my kids back home. It's too much bullshit going on out here. I'll be home as soon as I'm well enough to fly." I winced in pain as I spoke. It hurt to fucking breathe. Getting shot in the chest wasn't no punk.

"I don't know who the bitch is you're fucking down here, but I'm not going no motherfucking where. I'm your wife and as long as you're here in Chicago. I'm going to be here beside you. I know that things between us haven't been good in a long time but damn it Quaadir! You hate me that much that you don't want me around you?" Keesha was now crying and that was rare. No matter what went on between us, she never cried. She wasn't a weak bitch. She caught me numerous times cheating and she never showed her ass in public. What ever happened between us went on inside of our home. Keesha was really down for a nigga. She had been there when a nigga needed her most. I'd just gotten caught up in this lifestyle and the persona of being God. As I looked at her with tears streaming down her face, I could tell my actions were starting to wear her down.

"Come here, Keesh. Man, you know I love the shit out of you." I reached my hand out to her and she grabbed it. I pulled her in close and held her tight around the waist.

"You have a funny way of showing it. If I told you once I told you twice, if this is not where you want to be let me know. I'll take my daughters and leave your ass. I'm not with this crying shit."

"I also told your ass, I'm not going nowhere and neither are you. Stop threatening me with my girls. You know I don't play about my babies." Keesha always threatened to leave and take my kids away from me. Me and her both knew she wasn't going no motherfucking where. The day she took my kids away from me would be the day she became dead to me.

"Visiting hours are coming to a close. The girls are downstairs in the play area. I know that they are tired, so I'm going to go back to the hotel and get some rest. We're staying downtown at the Essex Inn. I'll be back in the morning. I love you, Quaadir." Keesh gave me a passionate kiss and walked out the room.

I took in her attire and how fucking bad she was. She was always on point when she stepped out the door. Not a hair out of place. Make-up on point. It wasn't a designer label my wife didn't own. Being the wife of the infamous "God" she had to look the part at all times. She had ass for days and a nice size rack that fit perfectly in my hand and in my mouth. Now that I sat back and thought about it, here it was I was lusting over another nigga's wife when I already had my own bad bitch at home.

Looking at her today made me want to reevaluate every fucking thing I had going on in the streets and at home. First thing first it was imperative that I get down to what the fuck was the real motive behind these people wanting Thug dead.

Chapter Five- Thug
Double Standards

Leaving Tahari on the floor crying like that was the hardest thing I ever had to do. Once I walked out of the door and got in my car, I shed tears like a motherfucker. No matter what type of Thug I was or the lifestyle I lived, Tahari was my weakness. Since she came into my life, she had made me a different man. I was nothing without her. As I lay in this fucking hotel room, all I could think about was that nigga Quaadir fucking my wife.

I was so fucked up about the shit that I had cut off communication with my entire family. I was so in my feelings right now that I didn't want to be bothered with nobody. I just wanted to clear my fucking mind. All I'd been doing was smoking and drinking, but all the fucking Kush and Remy in the world wouldn't take the pain away of my wife's betrayal.

Yes. I cheated on her and a part of me felt like her fucking dude was that shit that they called Karma. I didn't give a fuck how much a nigga cheated on his girl, the minute she fucked another nigga, all fucking bets were off. I was not a male chauvinist, but there was definitely a double standard when it came down to men and women. I think it hurts more because she lied about it. In my heart, I knew she was lying. I wanted her to tell the truth the first time I asked her ass. I wanted the truth, but when she told the truth, I couldn't handle it. I hadn't seen or spoken to her since I walked out and that was damn near two week ago.

Listening to Peaches crying on my voicemail made me feel even worse. I still hadn't spoke to her or seen her since the shooting. The last thing I wanted my mother to do was cry about me ignoring her. I was definitely going to give in and go to the family dinner she had arranged. Before I saw her, I needed to pay this nigga Quaadir a visit. I wanted that nigga six feet under so fucking bad, but I had to know who sent him and why. Plus, Peaches practically begged for this nigga's life. She knew I had every intention on finishing the fucking job. If this nigga valued life he'd better tell me what the fuck I wanted to hear.

****

I found out Quaadir's information from one my old chicks I used to fuck with. She just happened to be his overnight nurse. I checked my Desert Eagle as I exited my Bugatti. It had been so long since I drove that car. I actually missed it. I was dressed in all black from head to toe. I placed my gun in my waistband and headed towards the hospital's entrance. The lady working the front desk already had the heads up to let me up.

Quaadir's room was on the sixth floor. He was in the Intensive Care Unit and ole girl had already told me that he was up and talking. So, it was only right I paid his ass a visit tonight. I had my hoodie pulled down over my head and tied tight. Just in case some shit popped off. I opened his room door and he was sitting up watching TV. He looked over at me with a devilish grin.

"I knew you would be coming sooner or later," Quaadir said as he turned the TV off and turned to face me. I pulled my hood off of my head and sat down in the chair. I placed my gun on my lap so this nigga would know this shit wasn't a social call. There was no need for pleasantries.

"Let me cut straight to the fucking chase. Don't ever in your fucking life look at my wife or contact her for that matter. Whatever the fuck y'all had going on, that shit is a dead ass issue."

"Let me stop you right there. There is nothing going on between us. I admit I was feeling the shit out of her. She's beautiful as hell. What real nigga wouldn't want to fuck with her? She loves you and has made that perfectly clear. Even when you were supposedly dead."

I didn't feel the need to go in depth about their sexual encounter. Tahari had already told me enough. Plus, I would definitely blow his brains out if he got to describing her pussy and what it felt like.

"I'm glad you brought that up. Were you the trigger man in my shooting?"

"Yeah, that was me. I guess we're even since you hit me up." As I sat and looked at this nigga, I was starting to see a lot of Malik and myself in him.

"Actually, we're not even. I have a way of reading people and I know that you had no idea who I was. The only thing that's keeping me from finishing you off is my mother. It would break my heart if I had to break hers. So, I want to know who the fuck sent you at me and my family?"

As soon as the words left my mouth, the sound of gunfire erupting outside the door caused me to jump up and peep out the door. I watched as a tall white guy dressed in all black pinstriped suit held a gun to the nurse's head who helped me get in the hospital. I couldn't make out the words, but evidently she didn't tell him what he wanted to hear. He shot her right between the eyes. Her body instantly dropped to the floor. At that point, I noticed three more gunmen appear with guns in hand.

"What the fuck going on out there?" Quaadir asked. I turned around to look at him and he was now trying to stand up. The sound of another gunshot made me sprang into action. The gunshots were now in the distance. My antennas went up when I heard the gunmen going to other patients' room. I knew they were either looking for him or me. I wasn't in the mood to die tonight. I was about to do something I didn't come here to do and that was look out for my long lost twin brother. I needed this nigga alive in order to find out who was behind all the bullshit.

"Come on we got to get out of here!" At this point, he was already standing to his feet and ready to go.

"Damn! This shit hurt like a bitch." Quaadir was holding his chest and I started laughing like a motherfucker. I knew exactly how that shit felt.

"I guess I deserved that. All bull shit to the side though. How the fuck are we going to get out here without being noticed?"

"There is a exit door right next to this room. The sooner we get out of here the better."

We both slowly crept out of the door and headed towards the exit. The sound of gunshots in the distance could still be heard. As soon as we hit the stairs, the sound of security rushing the hospital floor could be heard. I looked back and Quaadir's ass was slow dragging. I wanted to leave his ass so bad, but I knew I couldn't. At any moment, the fucking hospital was about to be surrounded by Chicago's Finest. I was already out on bond and didn't have no time for this shit.

"You can't stop right now. I know that shit painful." Quaadir's ass had completely stopped running and looked like he was about to pass out. I was glad when we made it down to the first floor. I was thanking my lucky stars that I had parked in the space that I did. The police was starting to pull up in the front entrance. As soon as I lifted Quaadir into the passenger seat, I hopped in and got the fuck out of dodge.

"Nigga you look like you're about to die. I think I need to take you to another hospital," I said as I looked over at Quaadir; he was looking pale as hell and his bullet wounds were starting to bleed.

"Hell nah! That's the first place these motherfuckers gone look. Take me to my crib, so I can grab some clothes. Then you can drop me off at the Essex Inn on Michigan. That's where my wife and daughters are."

"Here call your wife and tell her we're on our way to pick her up. I can take y'all to one of our safe houses." This nigga had a whole family at home and was trying to take mine away from me. *His bitch must be ugly as hell*; I thought to myself.

"Thanks man."

"Don't thank me. Thank Peaches. Our mother saved your life. Plus, we still have unfinished business." The car was silent after that. I took Quaadir over to his crib and he grabbed some clothes. From there, I took him to pick up his wife and daughters. I was in shock when I saw his family. His wife was beautiful and stacked in all the right places. The thing that baffled me the most was that his twin daughter's looked like Ka'Jairea and Ta'Jay. That was really all the confirmation I needed that we were in fact twin brothers. I took them out to our vacation house on the Lake and got them settled.

"Nobody knows y'all are out here. I'll bring Peaches over in the morning to look after you. Don't try no bullshit. I got eyes on you." I had to let this nigga know don't try to pull a stunt like leaving town. Who ever wanted him to kill me now wanted his ass dead. I highly doubted he was going anywhere. Now, I just needed to put the family up on what the fuck is going on. I needed to go and see my wife and kids. I needed to make things right with Ta-Baby. I was missing the shit out of her.

Chapter Six-Tahari
Pieces of Me

It had been two weeks since Ka'Jaire left me all alone. The next morning after he walked out, I woke up in the same place he had left me. I had the worst headache ever. I struggled to stand to my feet. I knew that I couldn't lay around all day. Pretty soon my babies would be up and the last thing I needed was for them to see me crying and shit. I hopped in the shower and let the hot steaming waterfall all over my body. I wanted to cry so badly, but I didn't have any tears left.

"Momma eat-eat!" I pulled back the shower curtain and Kaine was standing there.

"Hey Baby. Momma will fix you breakfast in a minute." He sat on the floor and waited for me. Not long after, the whole gang was in my bed waiting for me. I couldn't do nothing but laugh as I stepped out of the shower and saw all of them. I got dressed in a hurry. I knew in a minute they would be going crazy due to being hungry.

It was a Sunday so I knew that we would be staying in the house for the day. Sundays were family day for us. We usually would go over to Malik or Ta'Jay's house for Sunday dinner, but I was too ashamed and embarrassed to be around the family. I knew that sooner or later I would have to face them. Today just wasn't one of those days.

All I wanted to do was spend time with my kids. We were going to eat junk food and watch movies all day. My kids were what I needed to take my mind off of Thug. Once they laid down for their naps, I had a minute to myself. I laid in bed and reflected on my entire relationship with Thug. He met me in my time of need and here it was three years later. I couldn't help but feel like he thinks I need him. My thoughts were interrupted by the sounds of Kaia and Kahari crying. They always woke up at the same time.

For the rest of the day, I catered to my kids and we enjoyed ourselves. I just hated that they kept asking for their father. I tried calling him several times and he never answered.

The next day I took Kaine to get his cast off. I was happy that everything had healed properly. I looked like the little old lady in the shoe with all these damn kids with me. I was glad that they were well behaved and dressed to the nines. Yes, my kids were dressed to impress whenever they stepped on the scene.

"Momma! I need to use the bathroom," Ka'Jaire Jr. said.

"Okay baby. Come on in the ladies room with me."

"I'm a boy. I'm not supposed to go in the girls' bathroom." He was fighting me to keep from going in the ladies room.

"You're definitely not going in the men's bathroom alone." I yanked his ass right in the bathroom with me. I didn't trust these sick ass people these days. When we entered the bathroom, there was a woman standing in front of the vanity crying.

"Is everything okay," I asked as I handed her some tissue to wipe her face.

"Thanks. I've been better."

"I hope everything works out for you."

"For the sake of my marriage. I hope everything works out, too."

"My marriage is struggling as well. My husband and me are going through some changes. I'm Tahari nice to meet you."

"Hey, I'm Keesha nice to meet you as well." We shook each other hands and continued to make small talk. The more we talked; I learned that she was at the hospital waiting on her husband's medicine. He had recently been released after being shot. I guess she became so overwhelmed that she had to go in the bathroom and let it all out.

"Momma, I'm finished."

"Okay. Wash your hands.'

"He's handsome. Is he your only one?"

"Girl no. I have six more in the lobby. Let me get out of here and get them home. It was nice meeting you, Keesha.

"Same here."

I rushed out of the bathroom and gathered up my babies. I needed to hurry up and get home. Trish was coming over for dinner and I hadn't prepared anything. Momma Peaches called me on the way home and told me that I could bring the kids to her house. Ever since Vinny had been called back to Miami on business, Peaches had been so lonely. I felt so sorry for Peaches when I dropped the kids off to her. With Vinny being so far away and the Quaadir situation, Peaches had become overwhelmed. I knew that her and me needed to sit down and talk about things. Peaches was putting on a brave front, but Thug not talking to her was breaking her heart.

*****

The soulful sounds of Mary J. Blige's *My Life* CD played throughout the house. I loved the fact that you could play that CD in its entirety. Mary J. Blige would have a bitch all in her feelings crying and shit. I sang along with Mary as I checked the Crab Legs I had boiling and the Shrimp that I had sautéing. I was so happy when Trish called and told me she was coming over. I definitely needed to talk to someone who had been through some things in their marriage.

Once the food was finished, I set the table and made sure our wine was on chill. Trish loved her some Sunset Blush wine. She had started me to drinking it and I was addicted. Once I changed into some jeans and a cut off shirt, Trish was calling me from the front gate letting me know that she had arrived. I typed in the code and met her out in the driveway.

"Hey Boo. What's up!" I said as we hugged each other and I escorted her inside.

"Damn! This shit is nice." I showed Trish around the house before sat down to eat. I poured each of us a tall glass of wine. We both started cracking open the crab legs and dipping them in the hot garlic butter.

"So, what's been up with you, Trish?"

"Same ole. Same ole. Keeping my shop running and of course being a wife and mother." I took a long gulp from my drink and zoned out for a minute. "Tahari! What are you thinking about over there?"

"I'm sorry girl. My life is falling apart. I hate to put a damper on our chill time, but Thug left me." I hurried up and wiped the tears before they fell.

"Oh, my God! I know he didn't leave because of this Quaadir situation. If he did he has a lot of fucking nerve."

"You know about me and Quaadir?" I was in shock because I thought no one knew.

"I hate to tell you this, but that shit is the talk of the family. Peaches called Gail crying and Gail can't hold hot water." I placed my head in my hands and I started to cry.

"I fucked up big time, Trish. How could I embarrass Thug like this? I don't know what I'm going to do. How can I look in his family's face knowing I fucked his brother?" Trish got up from her seat and came over to sit next to me."

"I'm going to keep this shit all the way one hundred with you. Tahari, the biggest mistake you're making right now is being worried about what they think. You're going to drive yourself crazy with guilt over something you shouldn't feel guilty about. You don't have no reason to be ashamed or embarrassed. You had no idea who he was."

"I just want to die Trish. I don't even think that you understand?"

"There's a lot about me that you don't know about. I been in your shoes before, so I know how you feel. Hell shit got so bad for me that I actually did try to kill myself. The problem is that we become so engrossed with who our husband's are ,that we forget who we are. That's why I grind so hard. I don't want to just be Markese's wife. I'm Trish that's it and that's all."

"It's funny you say that because I've been thinking that. All I am is Thug's wife. Since the day he picked me up battered and bruised, I've been up under him like a newborn baby. He has given me the world and I'm happy to be the mother of his children. Everyone looks at Thug like he's this great guy. Don't get me wrong, my husband is the total package.

He's every bitch's dream come true, but he's a typical nigga that does typical nigga shit. I swear when I walked in that room and saw him fucking that bitch, a part of my heart died. I never felt that I was capable of losing him to another woman. It doesn't matter that I go hard for him in these streets. I know now I'm not exempt from anything when it comes to our relationship. I came clean and told him that I fucked Quaadir. You should have seen his face. He looked at me with pure hatred in his eyes. I really think it's over."

The wine wasn't strong enough for me, so I got up and grabbed a bottle of Patron. We both started knocking shots back.

"Girl please, Thug ass ain't going nowhere. He somewhere kicking his own ass about you fucking Quaadir. The problem with men is they can fuck anything moving, but once we do it, it's the end of the world. He'll be home once he's over being mad, maybe even sooner. I know that Thug loves you. The last thing he wants is to see you with another nigga. Listen to me and listen to me good, stop crying and showing him you're weak for his ass. I know for a fact your ass ain't weak. All these bitches you've been bodying. You're more than just his ride or die bitch. You're his wife and the mother of his children. You have to give that nigga some act right and let him know you ain't playing with his ass."

For the rest of the night, we talked and laughed. I felt so much better after our talk. I was so fucked up from mixing that wine with Patron. I laid across my bed and went straight to sleep.

Chapter Seven- Thug
Putting Shit In Perspective

I dreaded going to talk to Peaches. I had put the shit off for so long that a part of me didn't want to face her. I still couldn't believe that I helped Quaadir out. I know for a fact I was about to get a lot of backlash from my crew. I did what I thought was best for everyone involved. Trust and believe me they would thank me later. I used my key and walked inside of Peaches' house. I found her in her favorite place; at the bar knocking back shots of Patron.

"Hey Ma." I walked over and kissed her on the cheek. I walked behind the bar and grabbed some Remy and a shot glass. Peaches never spoke back, so that meant she was mad at me.

"Ma. I know that you're mad at me for not answering your calls, but this shit fucked me up."

"Shut the fuck up, Ka'Jaire. You're so damn selfish. Did you ever stop and think about how this shit fucked the rest of us up? Yes, I kept another secret from my kids and that's something I have to deal with. I love all of my kids the same. I don't think you know it or not, but you're my rock Thug. You're the strongest out of all of us.

Without you, I can't function. I hate myself for never telling you that you had a twin."

"Don't worry about it Ma. All that shit is water under the bridge." Peaches narrowed her eyes at me as I spoke.

"Please tell me you didn't kill your brother, Thug." I saw her eyes get glossy like she was about to cry. That shit let me know that I couldn't kill his ass even if I wanted to.

"No, I didn't. That's actually why I'm here. I need you to pack some clothes and head over to the vacation house. Quaadir and his family are out there. I moved him from the hospital. Don't ask any questions. Just please go pack for me. I already hollered at Malik, Dro, and Sarge and they're aware of things." Peaches started shedding tears and hugged me so hard. She ran upstairs and got packed in no time. As we drove out to the vacation house, we made small talk and enjoyed each other's company.

"Have you talked to Tahari?"

"I really can't even look at her right now." I kept my eyes on the road because I could feel Peaches staring a hole through me.

"Go home to your family son. I know that it's hard knowing that your wife had sex with your brother, but the facts remains the same; neither one of them knew. Plus, Tahari is so heartbroken at home without you. I also know that you miss her and those kids."

"I miss her, Ma. I'm just having a hard time dealing with the fact that she slept with my someone else."

"I understand that you're hurt baby. How do you think she feels? She caught you having sex with another woman. When we all thought you were dead you were alive and fucking someone else. Let's not forget about the bitch Sabrina who was actually your cousin." Peaches grabbed the blunt from the ashtray and flamed it up. I swear my momma was a woman in a nigga's body.

"Please don't remind me." The last thing I wanted to think about was my dirt.

"I think that you need to be reminded. Mainly, because Tahari has taken a lot off of your ass. She deserves better from you than you to just walk out on her for one mistake." I never responded because I was letting my mother's words marinate in my mind. Once I dropped Peaches off, I headed straight home to see Tahari and my kids.

*****

I sat outside in my car before I went inside of the house. I looked up at our bedroom window and the light was still on. That meant Tahari was still awake. I laid my head back and thought about what I was going to say when I went inside. I smoked a whole blunt to the face and still had no idea what to say to her.

After about another thirty minutes, I gathered the courage and went inside. I headed straight upstairs. My first stop was to check in on my kids. They were all sleeping so soundly. The door to our bedroom was slightly cracked open. I pushed it open and walked in. Tahari was sitting up in bed with her upper body leaned against the headboard. As usual she was reading on her Kindle Fire. I noticed that she never even looked up at me. I went straight to the bathroom and took a shower. I was tired and all I wanted to do was climb in bed under Tahari. Maybe we could just talk about everything in the morning. Once I was done in the shower, I dried off and threw on a pair of basketball shorts. I grabbed the remote and cut on the TV to watch ESPN.

"What are you over there reading?" I asked her trying to break the ice. The awkwardness was between us was killing me. Tahari never even looked at me when she spoke. The next thing I knew she grabbed the comforter off the bed and stormed out the room. Everything inside of me told me to go after her, but my stubbornness wouldn't let me. I was tired as hell and eventually I drifted off to sleep.

****

"What the fuck!" I said as I jumped up trying to recover from being drenched in cold ass water.

"Really motherfucker? It's that easy for you to leave me for two whole weeks and return like it ain't shit. You got me and life fucked all the way up. Get your ass up and get the fuck out!" Tahari was standing at the foot of the bed holding a big ass pot.

"Why the fuck would you throw some cold ass water on me, Tahari?"

"Don't ask me no fucking questions. I packed you some clothes and they're by the front door. I came to the conclusion if it's that easy for you to walk out on me, then it won't be easier for you to just walk back in. I'm not beat to be your fucking doormat when I've treated you like the King you are. No matter how many times you cheated on me, I never walked out on you. I've always been there when you needed me. I apologized, I begged, and pleaded for your forgiveness. You walked out on me like I was bitch in the streets.

I have spent too much time trying to be the best wife to you, when I should have been the best woman I could be to myself. Not to mention, a fit mother to our kids. So, like I said get the fuck out!"

I just sat on the side of the bed and listened to Tahari vent. The shit she was saying had me thinking like a motherfucker. I was having hard time dealing with the fact that I was being put out the house my money bought.

"How the fuck are you going to put me out my shit?" I was now standing in face to face with Tahari.

"The same way you walked out the house willingly. Only this time, you're leaving by force. You're moving too slow." Tahari started to push me towards the door. It was taking everything inside of me not to lay hands on her. Instead, I knocked her hands off of me. I went inside the closet and took a couple of stacks out of the safe. I threw on a Nike jogging suit and a pair of all black ones. When I exited the closet, Tahari was still standing in the same spot I left her in.

"Why are you leaving again, Daddy?" Ka'Jairea asked as she rubbed her eyes. That shit ate me up because it had been a minute since I spent time with my kids. I felt so fucked up about everything.

"Mommy, thinks it's best that I move out. I promise I'll call and check on y'all every day. Be a good girl and help Mommy out okay." I wiped the tears from her eyes and I hurried up and left out the house. I would be fronting if I said I wasn't on the verge of crying right there with baby girl. Tahari had fucked me up in the head putting me out. She didn't shed a tear or think twice as she gave me my walking papers. My life was all fucked right now. I needed a stress reliever and I ended up in the last place I needed to be- with Yoshi.

Chapter Eight- Tahari
Done Playing Games

It took everything inside of me to stand my ground and make Thug leave. I wanted him and I yearned for him to be back home with his family. However, I knew he needed this wake up call. It bothered me that he would just come home and climb in bed with me, like he didn't walk out on me. As his wife, I felt like I deserved better than that.

I would have felt better if he would have at least came in kissing ass and bearing gifts, but his cocky ass came in with nothing. As I laid in the guest bedroom, I knew that I had to do something in order for him to take me seriously. I hated to put my kids in a predicament where they lived in a one-parent household, but I knew that I needed to do it. I was no good to my children if I walked around our house miserable because of Thug's presence. I hoped and prayed the shit didn't blow up in my face.

Instead of dealing with the things that were going on in my marriage, I focused on the opening of my nail bar. The Grand Opening was in two weeks and the girls and I were all putting in overtime making sure things went off without fault. I made sure not to call Thug for shit. I had my own bank account from the inheritance that I received from my grandmother and the money Cassie and Venom sent to me over the years.

I had everything that I needed to open and that made me feel so good. I had already done the hiring process for my nail techs and my barmaids. I felt so fucking liberated. Immersing myself in work helped me to deal with my family issues. I made it my business not to call or text Thug. If he wanted his family, he would show me by fighting for us. Since the night I put his ass out, I hadn't heard from him. That was fine by me because it was going to be a cold day in hell before I picked up the phone and called him. I hated to admit it, but I was done fighting for us because I always got hurt in the end.

The walls of my house were starting to close in on me and my kids. So I took them to the Golden Corral. I had them all sitting down while I grabbed the food of their choice.

"Hey girl. It is so crazy that we keep bumping into each other." I looked up and it was the young lady I had met in the washroom at the hospital.

"Yeah, it is. How are you doing?" I asked her as started making plates.

"It's okay I guess. I had to practically drag my husband out today. My girls were tired of being cooped up in the house." I watched as her daughters ran up to her and they were so cute. I couldn't believe she had a set of twins, as well.

"I didn't know you had twins girl. That's crazy because I three sets of twins." I pointed towards the table where my kids were.

"Yo',Keesh! What the fuck is taking you so long?" I dropped the plates of food that I had in my hand as I locked eyes with Quaadir. He had a shocked look on his face and Keesha had a confused look on hers.

"Is everything okay, Tahari?" Keesha asked as she started to help me pick up the mess I had made.

"Oh, yeah. I'm fine girl. I've been clumsy all day."

"This is my husband, Quaadir. Quaadir, this is Tahari. Remember I was telling you about the nice lady I met in the bathroom. Well this is her." Keesha smiled as she introduced us and we both did what came naturally to both us. We played that shit off like we had never met each other before. Quaadir was shaking in his fucking boots. He couldn't even look at me in my face.

All types of shit was flowing through my mind. This motherfucker was pursuing me like he was a single ass man. I didn't know why I was even surprised. This nigga had already showed me the real him. I was having a problem understanding why at that very moment of being in front of him and his wife was I feeling a little jealous. I hurried up and shook that shit off. It was his fault my damn marriage was falling apart. The sound of my children calling my name broke me from my thoughts.

"It was nice seeing you again and nice meeting you as well." I hurried and walked off. I felt so damn ashamed because in my head, I kept seeing the sexual encounter between Quaadir and I. As I sat and ate with my children, I found myself constantly looking over at the table that they were sitting at. Quaadir and I constantly kept stealing glances with one another. All I kept thinking about was Thug running up in here and shooting the damn restaurant up. I had to get the fuck out of dodge. My nerves was all over the damn place.

I gathered up my kids and we left the restaurant. When I made it home ,I called Barbie, Ta'Jay, and Khia. The bitches thought the shit was funny. It was nothing funny about the shit. I was confused because I didn't even know whether he was dead or alive. My thoughts drifted to Thug and where he could be. I was trying not to call him, but I knew that I needed to tell him about being out and bumping into him.

I called his phone and of course it went straight to voicemail. The inbox was full so I couldn't leave a voicemail message if I wanted to. I grabbed my Kindle Fire and I decided to read *Forever your Rider* by Shan and David Weaver.

My phone chimed alerting me that I had a notification on Facebook. I opened it up and I had to do a double take. It was a picture of Thug laying down in a bed sleep with a pair of Armani Exchange Boxer briefs on. The bitch Yoshi was laying on his chest. Her post simply read **#BaeAss**. I swallowed the huge lump that had formed in my throat. My heart was beating so fast. My feelings were so fucking hurt. Not because he was with another woman, but it was the woman he was with. This bitch was blatantly being disrespectful. I didn't even know we were friends to begin with.

People started commenting on her picture and it was none other than my bitches telling her how they was whooping her ass when they caught her. I chose not to respond. I was already looking like a fucking fool. I refused to give that bitch the satisfaction of seeing me sweat. I know that I put him out, so I knew that I ran the risk of him running to another bitch. I just hated that it had to be the one bitch I caught him in bed with.

I found myself constantly staring at the picture. I became so fucking angry. This bitch Yoshi really wanted me to kill her ass this time around. I immediately shook those thoughts from my mind. I was changing for the better. The days of me killing bitches behind my husband were over. My kids were my only concern. I needed a damn drink. I jumped up from my bed and went downstairs to grab a bottle of Moet from the fridge. I already had a blunt rolled and ready to be put in the air. As I sat up in bed and sipped, a text message came through and it was from Thug.

Hubby:I'm on my way to the crib. We need to talk about this Facebook bullshit

Me: There is nothing to talk about. Stay at that bitch house. I can't believe your trifling ass.

Hubby: Fuck all that. I'm on my way.

I sat up in bed and I flamed up my blunt. Not long after, I heard the front door open and close. The sound of Thug's footsteps coming up the spiral staircase made me get goose bumps. I had so many emotions going on inside of me. I was hurt, mad, and happy all at the same time. I hated the fact that I loved him so much. I also hated that he kept hurting me. As soon as he entered the room, my pussy did the same dance it did the first time I laid eyes on him.

For the life of me, I couldn't understand how this man's presence was so powerful. He was dressed in an all white button up shirt with a pair of all white True Religion jeans. He was rocking the hell out of an all white and gold Gucci gym shoes. His diamonds were blinding a bitch. Thug was looking sexy as fuck. I had to catch myself before he caught me lusting and staring at his dick print. I had to keep my game face on. I took a long pull from the blunt and eyed his ass like a hawk. If looks could kill he would be one dead motherfucker.

"Before you say anything, just let me explain," Thug said as he stood at the foot of my bed.

"I'm not about to say shit. At the same time there is really nothing for you to explain. A picture speaks a thousand words. I should have known you were still fucking that bitch. I should have killed both of you bitches when I had the chance!"

"I know that you're mad at me, but watch your motherfucking mouth. You of all people know ain't no bitch in my blood. I know how the shit looks and I'm sorry that you had to see that picture, but that bitch took that shit while I was sleep." Thug sat on the side of the bed and I jumped up and stood directly in front of him.

"Please explain to me why you were even in the bitch's presence."

"The night you put me out, I went over to her crib. I swear to God Bae, I didn't fuck her. I ended up falling asleep in her bed fully clothed. I sleep hard as and you know that. She took off my shit while I was sleep. That's how she got that picture of me. I'm so sorry,

Ta-Baby. I fucked up and let that bitch catch me slipping. I know that I have fucked up in the past, but I would never do no shit like that to you."

Thug was looking up at me with pleading eyes and all I could do was think about how fucking hurt I was. I also knew that he was telling the truth. One thing about Thug, he came clean about his shit. Once he was caught, he put it all out there.

"Why would you run to her? Out of all the bitches, why her?"

"I don't know, Ta-Baby." Thug put his head down in his hands. I grabbed his chin and made him look up at me so that we could look into each other's eyes. I was trying my best not to cry, but I couldn't stop the tears from falling.

"You don't love me anymore, Ka'Jaire?"

"Don't ever ask me no shit like that. I love you more than life itself. I hated to walk out on you like that, but knowing that you gave a nigga something that belongs to me fucked up my ego. You're mine and you belong to me. I will body you and any nigga that thinks he can have you. The only reason that nigga Quaadir is still breathing is because of Peaches."

"Listen to you, Thug. You're talking about me as if I'm a piece of property or one of your possessions. Not only am I your wife and the mother of your children--I'm a person, Thug, and I have feelings. In your eyes, I'm this ride or die chick that goes hard for her nigga. Underneath all of that, I'm a little girl longing to be loved and appreciated. Outside of you, your family and our kids, I have no one else. I admit I was wrong for sleeping with Quaadir and I was also wrong for lying about when you asked me the first time."

"I don't even want to think about you having sex with that nigga. So, let's just drop the subject." Thug grabbed the blunt from my hand and inhaled deep. He was running from the conversation, but I wasn't finished telling this nigga how his actions were affecting me.

"You don't want to think about me giving another nigga what belongs to you, but what about the fact that you're supposed to belong to me. You and this is my shit." I grabbed Thug's dick and held it tight as I continued to talk."Yet, you give it to other bitches as if you don't have the best pussy or million dollar mouth at home waiting for you. I never nag you or get in your business unless it's necessary. I know for a fact I'm a good mother and a wonderful wife. However, I know that you can't stop cheating on me. So, I made a decision." I walked over to my nightstand and got my wedding ring out and handed it to him.

"What the fuck you giving me this for?" Thug stood up from the bed and was now in my face.

"Obviously, this marriage is not working out. Let's just raise our children and move on with our lives."

"Stop fucking playing with me and put that ring on your finger. Don't make me fuck you up, Tahari. Fuck you mean this shit ain't working out. Starting now we're going to make it work and put all this shit behind us. As a matter of fact, I'm not about to keep playing with your ass. Bring that ass here."

Before I knew it, Thug had ripped my panties off of me and I had me lifted up in the air and leaned up against the wall. He had wrapped my legs around his neck and his mouth was assaulting my pussy. The shit was feeling so good all I could do was grab his head and pull his mouth in closer. I bit down on my bottom lip and let my head fall back. Thug was eating the soul out of my pussy and I was in pure ecstasy.

"Yasss Baby! Eat your pussy just like that," I moaned. I was holding Thug's head so tight and grinding into his face I was hoping I bruised his lips.

"You like this shit don't you?" he asked as he carried me over to the bed and positioned me on all fours. I felt his tongue slide up and down the crack of my ass. The feeling of his tongue dipping in and out of my ass hole had me rolling like I had popped a pill. The sound of Thug's jeans hitting the floor let me know what was next. Thug slowly and gently inserted the tip of his dick in my ass. I grabbed a pillow and braced myself for the pain and pleasure that was about to come. Thug went deeper inside of me and hit that spot that made me cum so hard.

"Oh, my fucking God! I love this shit, Ta-Baby." Thug said as he grabbed my hair. He pulled out and came all over my ass. He hit me on both of my ass cheeks. That shit drove me crazy and made me even wetter. He laid down beside me and guided me on top of him. I slid down on his dick without hesitation. I slowly rocked my hips back and forth as I rode him all the while sucking on his fingers.

"Whose dick is this?" I asked as I rode him hard and fast.

"This dick is all yours. It belongs to you." Thug roughly grabbed my hips and began thrusting in and out of me.

"Oh, shit Thug! I'm about to cum." I sped up the pace and began riding his dick like I was in the rodeo.

"Well cum then." He started to smack me on my ass and that was all she wrote; I creamed all over his dick. I collapsed on his chest out of breath. He rolled me over on my back and climbed on top of me. He inserted his dick back inside of me and he began to make love to me. He was giving me some of his Thug Passion.

"I love you, Ta-Baby."

"I love you too!" Not long after, Thug came harder than I ever saw him in all of our years together. He rolled off of me and tried to catch his breath.

"Now put that fucking ring back on your finger! Make that the last time you take it off," Thug said as he got up to go the washroom. I watched as his walked away. His body was glistening from the sweat that was pouring from his body. *It should be a sin and a shame for a nigga to be so fucking fine. I'm glad he's mine;* I thought to myself. I grabbed the ring off of the floor and placed it back onto my finger. Not long after, Thug came back into the room and climbed back into bed with me. He laid his head on my chest and I rubbed his back and his head.

"I missed you so much, Tahari. I promise I'm going to do everything inside of me to make shit right with us. I'm nothing without you, Tahari."

"I missed you, too. I don't want you to make anything up to me. As of right now, I just want us to be do better at this marriage and being better parents."Thug leaned up and kissed me so passionately. For the rest of the night, we made love to each other and made promises to one another that we both hoped we could keep.

Chapter Nine-Yoshi
I Need You Bad

It was mighty funny how every time Thug and his wife were going through shit, he ran straight to my fucking house. Not only had I been someone for him to vent to, I had also been some wet ass pussy for him to slide up in. I gave it to Thug however and whenever he wanted it. He could front for his wife all he wanted to, I've fucked her husband more times than she would like to know. Like the good obedient side bitch I am, I have never ratted on his ass and told her ass what the fuck had really been going on.

At first, it was just a fuck for me, but being around him more, I realized I wanted to be more than just some side bitch. I wanted Thug all to myself. I was so infatuated with him that I told all the other strippers to stay the fuck away from him. I would be the only bitch giving him lap dances and riding on that big ass Anaconda. I saw why his wife was so fucking crazy over his ass. That nigga knew how to lay that pipe and fixed all the fucking plumbing. I had to get used to his size. His ass had me walking bowlegged for days.

Shit was going so good for us. She just had to show her ass up at the club. Walking in her expensive ass clothes and shoes. Her ass was walking around like she owned the fucking place. I didn't own it, but I was top dog around that bitch. It really pissed me off as I watched her shake and gyrate her ass all over him. He made me even madder by trying not to acknowledge me, especially since we had just got off the phone making plans to meet up later that night.

I knew she was his wife and that was why I complimented her. She was fake as hell complimenting me on my Red Bottoms. She couldn't even hold a straight face when she spoke. I had to throw it out there that my boo bought them for me, but in actuality he had never bought me shit. I was in the process of trying to work my number on his ass. I saw him when he went in the bathroom and I made sure to follow his ass in there and lock the door.

I sucked his dick as if my life depended on it. I wanted to swallow his seed, but instead he let loose all over my face. I was so mad he did that shit, but I didn't show my anger. Once we exited the bathroom, I never even saw the bitch coming at me until I was on the floor. I still couldn't believe the bitch took my shoes. That was the only pair of Red Bottoms I had. After the fight I had no intentions on going with Thug, but once I got in the car with him, that shit quickly changed. I was definitely going to fuck him just to spite her.

The gunshot wound to the chest I received courtesy of her caused my fucking lungs to collapse. I had every intention on pressing charges on that bitch. Thug talked me out of it by giving me ten thousand dollars and one last fuck. I bet his wife didn't know about that. After that last time, he cut all ties with me. It had been a minute since I had heard from him. It was in his absence, I wanted him in my life. I yearned for him at night when I masturbated, wishing my fingers was his dick. I slowly started to get used to the fact that our little fling was over.

Out of the blue, he called me and showed up at my door drunk as fuck and looking a hot ass mess, but still sexy as hell though. I let him in and led him to my bedroom. I was definitely getting me some that dick. As soon as he hit the bed, he was out like a light. This nigga knew he slept hard as hell.

I undressed him and he didn't feel a thing. That was until I started playing with his dick, and knew then he was definitely drunk when he started calling me Tahari. I made sure to use that shit to my advantage. I put it in my mouth and went to town. I was mad as hell because his shit would not get erect for nothing in the world. I even tried to put it inside of me while it was soft and nothing happened. I was so mad at his ass. I just decided to take a fucking picture and tag the bitch in it. Served her ass right for shooting me in the first fucking place.

Not long after he woke up and went back to his hotel. He just got up, put his clothes on, and walked out like it wasn't shit. This nigga was cocky as hell. Who the fuck did he think he was to cause all this drama in my life? I was so over his ass. He wasn't getting out fast enough. I couldn't wait until that bitch saw that picture. I hoped and prayed I crushed her heart and soul. Her ass was so in love with his ass. The bitch had no clue how he passed out the dick.

Not even an hour after he left, he was blowing my phone up, but I refused to answer. I pressed ignore and sent his ass straight to voicemail. When I finally did listen to the voicemails ,he had left me a few choice words and death threats, which I knew he had no problem acting on. It was then I decided to get to him first. If I couldn't have him, neither could that bitch or all them damn BeBe Kids.

Chapter Ten- Keesha
Everything Comes to the Light

I'm so sick and tired of Quaadir and all the bullshit that came with being married to his ass. I loved my husband lord knows I do, but I didn't know how much more a bitch could take. I watched as I introduced Quaadir and Tahari to one another. The way they looked at each other let me know that they already knew each other. My feelings were so hurt as I watched Quaadir constantly looking over in her direction. He acted as if his children and me were not sitting at the table with him. I was so happy when she left the restaurant. It was only then that I had his undivided attention.

It took everything inside me not to stab his ass in the heart as he sat across from me. For the rest of the day, I didn't want to speak or even see Quaadir's ass. I should have stayed my ass in Atlanta. I felt like I was being held captive by Thug's ass. I didn't know what was going on with him and Quaadir, but some shit was not adding up. You would think after finding your long, lost twin brother their ass would be happy, but that was not the case at all. They acted like they hate each other.

I was glad Peaches had been keeping me company. She was so crazy. My girls loved the fact that they finally had a grandma to call their own. They have had Aunt Ruth, but she didn't want them calling her grandma. I was glad to see Peaches and Quaadir getting along better. Quaadir tried to act all hardcore, but I knew that it warmed his heart to finally know who his birth mother. I loved how Peaches had welcomed us into her family.

Since I'd been around her, I'd thought about my mother and whether she was alive or not. That bitch better hope she was dead because if we ever crossed paths, I was going to kill her ass. I knew my father was somewhere lurking in the shadows looking for me. They probably both are. I hadn't seen either one of them in eleven years.

I grew up in Miami, Florida. I never really knew what my parents' line of work was. I knew that my father had various businesses around the town. I had everything a little girl would ever want and need. To the outside world, I had it made, but behind closed doors I was enduring unspeakable horrors at the hands of my parents.

Since the age of eight, my father raped and sodomized me on a daily basis. He was so fucking brutal. I tried telling my mother what he was doing to me, but she told me that I shouldn't fight him and if I laid there and be still, he would be gentle with me. I hated her guts from that day forward. What type of mother sits back and allows her husband to molest their child? After years of sexual abuse at the hands of my father, I became pregnant with his baby at the age of fourteen. It was then I knew that I had to get as far away from them as I could.

My father had told me the code to his safe just in case something happened to him or my mother. As I sat and planned my escape, I knew that I needed to get some money in order for me to survive. I waited until they both left one morning and I hit the safe. I grabbed stacks of money without even counting and I got the fuck out of dodge. I brought a one-way ticket to Atlanta and I never looked back. A chance encounter led me into the arms of Quaadir. But, that's a different story for a different book.

****

"Ahhhh! That shit hurt, Keesh,"Quaadir yelled out in pain as I changed his bandages on his wounds. I was being rough as hell on purpose. I snatched the tape off of his chest even rougher when Tahari's face flashed in my mind.

"Get the fuck off me! Your ass doing that shit on purpose." Quaadir pushed me so hard that I fell back into the dresser. I pounced on ass without hesitation.

"Nigga don't put your fucking hands on me. I bet if I was that Tahari bitch you wouldn't be doing me like this." I was hitting his ass and he was trying his best to block the blows. I knew he was weak, so I used that shit to my advantage. I guess I got a little too carried away because I swung and it landed on one of his wounds. He backhanded my ass with so much force that I swear I felt my whole face shift to the other side.

My nose and the inside of my mouth was bleeding. I sat down on the side of the bed and held my head back to stop the blood from flowing. I wasn't mad that he hit me. That shit was a normal thing for us. We always had physical fights.

"What the fuck is you on with me, Keesha?" Quaadir came and sat next to me. He was holding a towel up to my nose. I took it from him and went inside the bathroom and I locked the door. I slid down to the floor and all I could do was cry. I made sure to cut the water on so that it could muffle my cries. I made it a habit to never cry in front of him. It showed signs of weakness. It was bad enough he cheated constantly and I forgave him every time. Mainly because he was all I had as far as family, but I didn't know how much longer I could deal with his bullshit. My love for him and my daughters were the only thing keeping me here.

After I got myself together, I took a shower and climbed into bed. Quaadir was already in bed. I pulled the covers up over me and turned my back to him. I felt him wrap his massive arms around my waist.

"I'm not going to be able to fix things if you don't tell me what the fuck got you so mad at me." I rolled over in bed and stared in his beautiful eyes before I spoke.

"How long have you been fucking, Tahari? Please don't lie. I watched the way you looked at her today. You looked at her the way that you used to look at me. I'm not stupid, Qua. You and her have known each other way before I introduced y'all. Do us both a favor and keep this shit one hundred. It's bad enough you make a fool out of me back in the A, but you shitting on me here in Chicago as well."

"There is nothing going on with me and her. That's Thug's wife. I've been down here to kill him, but shit got all fucked up for me down here. I had to use Tahari to get closer to him. In the process, one thing led to another and we did have sex, but this was before we knew that Thug and I was related."

"So, that explains why y'all beefing so hard. I can't believe all this shit is over pussy. I'm so fucking done with this shit. I'm going home after the dinner at Peaches' house. As far as I'm concerned you can stay your ass here. I want a divorce." I jumped out of the bed and tried to walk out, but Quaadir blocked me.

"Get the fuck out of here with all that divorce bullshit. I fucked up and I know that. Please don't leave, Keesh. Let me make this shit right. You can't go home anyway it's too much bullshit in the air. I need you here beside me. It's some major shit about to go down."

"I'm fed up, Qua. I can't do this shit no more. Please let me go!" I was trying my best to get out of his arms. On the other hand it felt so good. It had been so long since I felt his touch. We'd been fighting since I got here. Quaadir pushed me back on the bed and dropped down to his knees. He slid two fingers inside my pussy and played with my clit at the same time. He gently began to suck on my inner thighs. He slowly and methodically made love to my pussy with his mouth. I was squirting all over the damn place.

"Please don't stop, Quaadir. Oh, my God I missed this shit." Quaadir stood up and let his boxers fall to the floor. I bit down on my bottom lip as he slid his hand up and down his already hard member. He climbed in between my legs and plunged his dick into my pussy. I was so wet it felt like he was swimming in my shit. He was roughly thrusting in and out of me. I grabbed his face and started to kiss him. I tasted all of my juices as our tongues found one another. His dick was feeling so good that I momentarily forgot that we were fighting minutes earlier.

"You still want a divorce?"

"No," I moaned out in a low tone.

"You staying here with your husband right?" He pulled his dick all the way out and dived back in with so much force I swear I felt in my damn throat.

"I'm staying here with you baby!" I yelled out so loud I was pretty sure I woke up my daughters. Not long after, we came at the same time. I just laid there trying to get my thoughts together. The only sound that could be heard in the room was Quaadir breathing heavily.

"I promise I'm gone make this shit right, Keesh. Just stick it out with a nigga. I know I don't deserve it, Baby, but I need your support." Quaadir rolled over and kissed me on the lips. I returned the favor. As much as I wanted to protest, I didn't have the heart to.

In my heart I knew I wasn't leaving my husband. I had been through too much with his ass. It had been a long time since I stood beside my man and let my trigger finger do the talking. I needed to come out of retirement. These bitches sleep on me and over the years Quaadir forgot I was not to be fucked with. He knew for a fact it was going to take more than a good dick down to make me feel better. He just awakened the sleeping beast that he created.

Not to mention, I needed to have a sit down with this bitch Tahari. I already knew that with her being Thug's wife, eventually we would have to be in each other's presence. I was not beat for fucking with fake bitches, so we were going to have to get some shit straight. She needed to stay away from my husband because I had no problem with throwing the pussy at Thug with his fine ass.

Chapter Eleven- Thug
The Kenneth Brothers

With all the bullshit that had been going on, I had yet to meet up with my team and let them know about this Quaadir situation. It was the night of the family dinner and I knew that I needed to tell them about helping this nigga out of that jam. I arranged for all of us to meet up at the warehouse. I wanted this shit to take place prior to the dinner because Quaadir and his family would most definitely be attending.

Quaadir and I were already at the warehouse waiting for Malik, Dro, and Sarge to arrive. Since the day I took him to the vacation house, I had been stopping by just to get a feel for his ass. After doing some research, I found out he was big shit in Atlanta. He was in my neck of the woods now. I was the only nigga that was big shit around these parts. I had held off on asking who sent him because I wanted my crew to be present.

We sat in silence as we passed a blunt back and forth between us. One thing I liked about him, he never showed his hand; here he was getting ready to meet niggas that had been gunning for him, and he was laid back cool, calm, and collective. He definitely was my brother. I made sure to never act as though I was ecstatic about him being my twin. My goal was to find out why he was gunning for me first.

"The Money Team is here!" Dro yelled as he entered the warehouse with Malik and Sarge behind him.

" What's up nigga spit that hot shit now?" Malik was on straight beast mode. One thing about my little brother when he was at a nigga's head, he followed through with all threats. I looked over and Quaadir had upped his Desert Eagle.

"Put that shit up, both of y'all. We're here on business. Put all that rah-rah shit to the side for a minute.

"Fuck all that. Nigga you had that bitch kidnap my motherfucking son!" Before I knew it, Sarge gave Quaadir a quick ass combo. He recovered and threw some punches back. Before they could really get to humbugging, me and Dro pulled them a part. Malik's ass was standing there laughing as he smoked a blunt.

"I didn't have shit to do with no fucking kidnapping. I didn't even know the bitch had done the shit. That wasn't a part of what the fuck I came here to do. Let's get this shit over with. I need to get back to wife and kids."

"Calm the fuck down everybody! I called this meeting so that we can put all the bullshit on the table. As you all know Quaadir is my twin brother and your brother Malik." I looked over at Malik and gave his ass a stern ass look because I knew he was getting ready to say some smart shit. "I know that we're all running off emotions and adrenaline, but in order for us to get to the bottom of this shit we need to put all our egos to the side and our guns on the table."

We all went around the table one by one and put our guns on the table. I could tell that my crew wasn't feeling this shit. I didn't give a fuck; I was still the head of this fucking family and I called the fucking shots. With respect to the fact that they held me down no matter what. I gestured towards Quaadir for him to take the floor and let us know what was really good.

"I was contracted by the Gianelli Crime Family to take you out, Thug. I never ask questions. I just do my hit and keep the fuck moving. Besides having the A on lock, I'm also a contract killer. Before I even came into contact with your family, I had pictures of all of you coming and going. I'm not sure what you did to Don Gianelli, but that nigga want you out of the picture. We're all men here and I'll be the first to admit that Tahari was my target to get closer to you. I went a little too far--" I cut that nigga off in mid sentence. Just hearing him say my wife's name had me wanting to reach for my gun and blast his ass.

"You can skip over that part. Don't even let her name roll off your tongue," I said as I opened a fifth of Remy.

"If I had known that y'all was my blood, I never would have came at y'all on this bullshit. I would have murked that fat motherfucker on sight."

"Have you ever heard of Vinny Santerelli?" Malik asked as he knocked back a shot of Remy. He was giving Quaadir the death stare. I felt like a proud father. I had trained my brother to become a ruthless goon and let a motherfucker know not to fuck with him.

"I never heard of him before. Why? Is he someone I should now?"

"He's our father. For a minute I thought he was behind all of this shit. On some real shit, we need to get at the motherfucking Gianelli's. Are you riding for your blood or nah? It would break Peaches heart if you weren't riding for your blood," Malik said as he continued to stare Quaadir down.

I sat back and let my Lil Bro run the show. I had been thinking of handing over everything to him. I was ready to get out of the game. I needed to be a better husband to Tahari and a better father to my seeds. Malik just showed me that he could run this shit without me. After we off these motherfuckers who want me dead, I was out of the game. That was a wonderful feeling; I'll be damn near thirty years old and retired.

"I always wanted to know who my mother was. Now that I have her in my life, I would never go against her. Despite the beef that we have amongst each other, I'm glad I have two brothers and a sister. I grew up an only child and that's a lonely ass existence. Just know that my shit stay cocked and ready to go. When y'all letting off shots, trust and believe, I'm letting my shit blow right beside you." That statement solidified our newfound brotherhood and the streets wasn't ready for the Kenneth brothers. We were a force to be reckoned with. The Gianelli Crime Family wasn't even ready for the bloodshed headed their way.

"I think this calls for a toast. That beef shit is over, we're a family now. The world is ours and as long as we rock for one another. We will forever and always be Kings of these streets. Let's get this money and off the motherfucking Gianelli Family. They want to go the war with me? Well a war is what we're going to give them."

We clinked our glasses and knocked our shots back and dapped one another up. All that beef shit was behind us. We needed to focus on the motherfuckers who was trying to bring down the empire my mother started.

"Let's get the fuck out of here. Peaches will have a fit. If we're late." We all left the warehouse and headed over to her house. I knew that I had made the right decision by allowing Quaadir to live and be a part of our lives. He just better stay the fuck away from my wife. I wouldn't hesitate to put a bullet in his ass.

Chapter Twelve- Peaches
Family Dinner From Hell

The night of my family dinner had finally come. I went all out to make sure that everything was perfect. I cooked greens, baked macaroni, ham, turkey and dressing, lasagna, chitlins, fried chicken, and potato salad. For dessert I had sweet potato pie, Red Velvet cake, German Chocolate cake, and of course cupcakes for my grandbabies. I had everything set up so neat and perfectly.

The adults were going to sit at one table and the kids had their own table. The only thing was missing was my husband. Over the course of this last year, he had shown me that he regretted walking away from me and my kids. It'd been a long time since I loved someone. I could honestly admit I loved Vinny and I was so happy I said yes. He had been the best father in the world to not only my boys, but to my baby girl. My grandbabies loved their paw paw. He was so in love with them that they each had their own college bank accounts with ten thousand dollars in it and counting.

When he first went away on business to Miami, I was skeptical because he had become distant, but I gave him the benefit of the doubt and trusted his word. I was skeptical but I let go and let him do him. I knew that being the Don of the Santerelli Crime Family required a lot of his time. I'd never been the type of woman to nag a man and I wasn't about to start now. I was so happy when he called and said he would be home soon. He needed to tell me something. That was fine by me because I had yet to tell him about Quaadir. I was so happy Quaadir had finally came around and was trying to build something with me. This dinner was a new beginning for our whole family.

"You got it smelling too good in here, Ma. I'm about to max something," Ta'Jay said as she rubbed her stomach. Ever since she became pregnant, her ass has been eating like a horse.

"I hope you made me my own Sweet Potato Pie."

"Yes, I did with your greedy ass. It's not just for you. It's for my grandbaby and Sarge, too." I watched as she took the sweet potato pie and put in her big ass Birken bag. I had never seen no fat shit like that in my life. All I could do was laugh.

Not long after Barbie, Tahari, and Khia had arrived along with the kids. I couldn't wait for Keesha to arrive with my Lil Mommas. Ka'Jairea was going to be so happy that she had girl cousins her age. Tahari, Barbie, Ta'Jay, and Khia were so close. I wanted them to welcome Keesha into their circle. She'd been through a lot and she needed some girlfriends that she could get into some bullshit with.

"Let's eat. I'm hungry as hell," Thug said as he came through the door with the Malik, Sarge, Dro, and Quaadir. Keesha and the girls came in as well. She was so pretty and I knew that she would fit in as well. I just hoped her and Tahari wouldn't be on no beef shit about no dick. I wanted them to let that shit go.

"Damn Ma! It's looking like Thanksgiving in this bitch," Malik said as he stole some chitlins out the pot.

"Get the fuck out my pots and wash your hands. Go sit your black ass down." I started to fix everyone's plate and it was time for us all to sit down and eat, but I needed to make a speech beforehand.

"I'm so happy that my family is here and we all as one. I feel so elated that my son Quaadir is finally here sitting in his rightful place amongst his family. I'm grateful that I gained another daughter-in-law in Keesha and two more grandbabies."

I watched as Keesha was staring at Tahari as if she wanted to jump across the table and hit her. I observed Barbie, Ta'Jay, and Khia staring Keesha down. That let me know that she knew about Tahari and Quaadir. At first, I wanted to just sit back and let them stare each other down, but if it was beef we were about to address the shit. As soon as I was about to call their asses out on the bullshit, the doorbell rang. My entire family was here, so I wondered who could be at my door.

"I know how y'all feel about my mother, but I think that she has changed for the better. I invited her. Please, Peaches, don't be mad at me. I'm trying to build relationship with her." If I didn't love Tahari I would have probably beat the fuck out of her for inviting that bitch to my house. I watched as she ran and opened the door for the bitch Cassie.

As she stepped into my house, I had the right mind to beat blood out this bitch. She walked in with the biggest smile on her face. That smile wasn't on her face that long because Keesha pounced on her ass and started beating the fuck out of her.

"You Bitch! I hate you!" Keesha kept saying over and over again as she hit Cassie. I watched as Tahari pounced on Keesha and they started to fight. I mean blow for blow. Khia, Barbie, and Ta'Jay were trying their best to jump in it. I was glad their husbands were holding them back. Finally, Thug and Quaadir was able to break them up from fighting. Cassie was on the floor bloody as hell. Keesha had beat the fuck out of her ass in a matter of seconds

"Why would you do that shit, Keesha?" Quaadir asked as he tried to hold her back.

"That's my mother. She let him hurt me, Qua," Keesha said over and over again as she fought to get out of his grasp. Tears were streaming down her face.

"What the fuck are you talking about? That's my mother," Tahari said as she was trying to fight and get to Keesha. Thug could barely hold her back.

"Well, then we're are sisters because that's my poor excuse for a mother. So, we share mother's and dick too. You fake ass bitch I know you and my husband was fucking around." Quaadir grabbed Keesha and pushed her towards the back of the house. She fought him like a rabid animal. That girl looked like she wanted to kill Cassie and Tahari's ass.

"Is is true Cassie? Is that my sister?" Tahari asked as Thug still continued to hold her. Tears were streaming from her eyes as she stared at Cassie.

"Yes, she's your sister." We all just stood there speechless as Cassie stood up from the floor and walked out the door like it was nothing. That bitch was worse than me. I was glad she left because I owed her an epic ass whooping for all of the drama she caused. I didn't have no Lipton but the Patron bottle I had was just fine. I needed to get drunk behind the shit that just transpired. All I wanted was a nice family dinner. Who the fuck was I kidding? There was nothing nice about this family.

"I wish I would have caught that shit on camera. I would have put that shit on World Star," Barbie said and I gave her ass a look that said shut the fuck up. Right now was not a time for jokes. Tahari was really upset and Thug was trying his best to console her.

"I told you Cassie wasn't shit, Ta." Thug wiped the tears from her eyes.

"I know, but I just wanted to get to know her. Can we please go home?"

"Hell no, you can't go home. I slaved over a hot ass stove all day long to make sure that we had a great dinner. Now, I suggest you go get it together and talk with Keesha. They're apart of this family now. I know it's hard to get used to them being around, but we have no other choice. Before we leave this house today we will all be on good terms. Whatever happened in the past will stay there."

"I'm actually glad I have another brother. I get to get spoiled times three. I hope y'all schooled him on me. I get whatever I want when I want it."

"Yeah, I got that memo, Lil Sis," Quaadir said as him and Keesha came back into the dining room. I had tears in my eyes as I watched everybody embrace Quaadir. Keesha and Tahari just stood and stared at each other.

"I'm sorry I disrespected your home, Momma Peaches."

"You don't have anything to be sorry about. I'm glad that you whooped her ass because if you hadn't, I was going to fuck her ass up. We are all hungry. Let's just sit down and eat right now."

I felt so bad for Keesha and Tahari because they deserved a mother that would love them and put them first. I might have secrets, but I showed my kids love and affection. They didn't have to worry about anything. As long as I was alive and breathing, I would be a mother to them. I was going to do my best and get them to come together. I just hoped and prayed they didn't kill each other first.

Chapter Thirteen- Tahari
Long Lost Sister

I had been calling Cassie's phone over and over again. She refused to answer for me. How could she not tell me that I had a sister? No matter how good things were going there was always some bullshit lurking in the shadows. I couldn't believe that she just walked out of the door like that. No explanation or nothing. I really thought that our relationship could be repaired. Now I knew that it couldn't. I should have listened to my husband.

I was really bothered that everyone was getting along with Keesha and Quaadir. I guess it was because my ass was uncomfortable. I fucked my husband's brother, which happened to be my sister's husband. This was some Jerry Springer shit. Thug and Quaadir was acting like the best of friends and the shit was sickening. Not to mention this bitch Keesha kept staring me down. I swear we could go for a round two if that was what she wanted. I was not trying to fight with her ass though. I just kept hearing her say that she let him hurt her. I wondered what she meant by that.

Thug had been really supportive since the incident at Peaches' house. I was glad he never said I told you so. I had been laying in bed for two days. I was trying to wrap my mind around my shitty ass life.

"Get your ass out the bed. You're meeting up with Keesha to do some shopping," Thug said as he came out of the bathroom with a towel wrapped around his waist.

"What the fuck are you talking about? I didn't get that memo. I'm not going anywhere with her."

"This is not up for discussion. Get your ass up! You need to sit down and talk with her, Ta-Baby. That's the only way you'll feel better." Thug let the towel drop to the floor and I wasn't paying attention to shit he was saying. I wanted some of that dick. I crawled to the edge of the bed and tried to taste it.

"You're on a punishment. Your ass ain't getting none of this good shit until you get your ass up and meet up with your sister."

"Really, Thug?" I couldn't believe he was trying to keep the dick from me.

"Dead ass." Thug walked away from me and started to get dressed. I was too mad at his ass. I got out of bed and started to get dressed. I only did because I wanted some dick. I couldn't wait to get his ass back. It took me about an hour to get dressed.

"Why are you dressed like you're going to fight?" Thug asked as came downstairs.

"Just in case that bitch jump stupid."

"Come here, Ma. Don't go in there on bullshit. Promise me that you won't fight with Keesha." Thug had grabbed me around my waist and pulled me in close. He was placing soft kisses on my neck.

"I promise."

"That a girl. When you come home, I'll have this cock hard and ready for you." Thug smacked me on the ass and I walked out the door. I said a prayer as I drove to The Water Tower to meet up with Keesha.

****

"I'm glad that you came to meet up with me. I know that it must be hard finding out you have sister after all these years," Keesha said as we walked around Victoria Secret.

"Yeah, it's hard." I was short with my answers because I knew that she really wanted to know about Quaadir and me. In order for us to come to terms with us being sisters, we would have to deal with what happened between Quaadir and me.

After we shopped for another hour, we decided to head over to the Grand Lux Cafe for lunch. The silence between us was so awkward as we looked over the menu. Instead of us ordering food, I ordered a double shot of Patron and she ordered a double shot of Hennessy. I decided to talk about the elephant in the room.

"I'm sorry about what happened between me and Quaadir. It was only one time. I regret it every day because I almost lost Thug over it."

"Did you know he was married?"

"No, I had no idea. If it's any consolation he was only dealing with me to get to Thug. Now we all know what's really going on. You don't have anything to worry about. There is nothing going on between Quaadir and I. I love my husband."

"I love my husband as well. I'm glad to know that whatever y'all had is over. I've been through so much in my life. The only thing I have in this world is my husband and my girls." I listened as Keesha spoke and we were both rocking in the same boat. I couldn't help, but console her as tears fell from her eyes. She began to tell me how Venom raped her and Cassie let him. The more we talked, the more we learned from each other about our evil parents. I never wanted to see Cassie's ass again. I learned that I was two years older than her.

"Now that we know about each other. We need to make a pact to always be there for one another. All we have is each other." We hugged each other and continued to drink and get to know each other.

"Where is Venom?"

"Let's just say he can never hurt us again." I was so happy that we were able to sit down and act like adults. At first, I definitely expected her to pop off about what happened between Quaadir and I. As we spoke, I realized that he never told her that he pursued me for a damn year and it definitely wasn't business. Considering the fact that we're all family now, I didn't feel the need to go in depth about things. It was water under the bridge and I wanted to keep it that way. I was so glad I gained another sister.

"I observed how you came to Cassie's rescue that night. Let me be the first to tell you. Watch that bitch, she is only out for herself. I lived in the house with her for fourteen years. The only person Cassie loves is herself. She's so selfish. It's real fucked up that she never told either of us about having a sibling. I hope and pray I see her ass before I go back to Atlanta. I'mma kill her ass." Keesha knocked back her shot without blinking an eye. I knew she meant every word she had said.

Chapter Fourteen- Khia
Undeserved Karma

All I wanted was to be happy and raise my son. He deserved to grow up and have a happy life. Nico's mother Lisette had been harassing me and constantly threatening to take Khiandre away from me. There was a point where I started to feel bad and I was going to let her see him. She was his grandmother after all and I didn't want to take him from her. The fact that she was clean was a plus in her favor.

Dro would kill me if he knew that I allowed our son to visit with Lisette. The visit was going good until she found out that I changed my son's name. She started cursing me out and being disrespectful. I took my son and I left her house. That was the last time I ever saw her. I was recently served with custody papers. This crazy bitch was suing me for custody of my son. Not to mention her ass was constantly running to the damn police saying that I knew who killed Nico. I was sick and tired of this damn Detective Jones harassing me. There had been so much going on with Thug and his family that

I had yet to tell them what was going on. Dro was aware of it, but lately he seemed to be so preoccupied.

I knew that I had no business going through Dro's phone. I just had to see if he was cheating on me. I hoped and prayed that he wasn't. That shit would surely break my hurt and get him fucked up behind it. To my surprise, he had a lock on his shit. That was a sign telling me to leave the shit alone. He had never had a lock on it before and all of sudden it was locked. That shit could only mean one thing; his black ass had something to hide.

I heard him flush the toilet, so I hurried and laid his phone back down. Lately, it had been bothering me that I had never met his children before. He had two girls and one boy with his ex-girlfriend Keshauna. I had never had a problem with her. Not even back in the day when he was her man and I was messing around with him. Not too long ago, I found out he had been cheating on me with her. I sliced his ass and he promised that it would never happen again. However, I think that something was still going on.

"Baby, I was thinking you should bring your kids over here, so that I can meet them. It would be really good for Khiandre to get to know his brother and sisters."

"Now, is not a good time, Khia."

"Well, when is a good time because you've been using that line all year. Let me find out!" He was pissing me off always using this lame ass excuse.

"Let you find out what, Khia. Don't start this shit. I'll let you meet my kids when I'm ready for you to meet them." I know this nigga didn't just say what I think he said.

"Fuck you and your kids." I jumped out of that bed and tried to walk fast as hell out of the room. I didn't make it far because Dro had pushed me in my back so hard it caused me to stumble forward and fall face forward. I put my arms up in front of me to break the fall. The sound of my bone breaking echoed loudly.

"Don't you ever say no shit like to me. Would you like it if I said fuck you and Khiandre?" I shook my head no because the pain was so unbearable that I could barely speak. I used my good arm to stand up. Dro had already walked away and left out of the house. I knew that I had broke something.

I was unable to drive, so I called Tahari to come and take me to the hospital. I was shocked when she came through the door with Keesha. I was sitting at the bottom of the stairs rocking my baby back and forth. Trying not to focus on the pain.

"What the hell happened, Khia? Where the fuck is Dro?" Tahari rushed in and grabbed Khiandre out of my arms. Keesha helped me off the stairs and we walked out the car. I had yet to answer her question and I prayed she didn't ask me again.

When we made it to the hospital, they took me straight to the back to be checked out. Just like I expected, my damn arm was broke in two places. Once it was casted, I was informed that I was ten weeks pregnant. I was in shock because I was still getting a period and didn't have any morning sickness. I sat on the bed and cried for so long. The pain meds that they had given me had me woozy. All I wanted to do was sleep.

"I'll take Khiandre home with me. You go home and get some rest. We'll come by and check on you tomorrow. Don't think I'm stupid either. You better tell me the truth about what happened to your fucking arm." I wasn't in the mood for Tahari and her bossiness right now. I just wanted to go home and get some sleep.

****

The sound of someone banging on my door woke me up from my sleep. I laid there as long as I could. I finally got up from the bed and answered the door. I stood there speechless as Dro's baby mother stood on my damn porch. Her ass better be lucky my arm was in a damn cast because my hands would be wrapped around this bitch's neck.

"Can I help you with something?" I asked this bitch because she was looking like she wanted to jump stupid.

"Where the fuck is Dro at?"

"Pipe the fuck down bitch. Don't come to my fucking house being disrespectful. He's not here right now and I'm quite sure you have his number. I suggest you use it before you pop up at my doorstep." I was trying to slam the door on this bitch, but she pushed the door back with force. I never even saw the knife until she started to stab me repeatedly. I never had a chance to react. She kept stabbing me in my stomach. I fell down to my knees and she straddled me. With my good arm I was trying to fight her off, but that only caused her to stab me even more. I also felt her stabbing me in my arm as well.

"Die Bitch! You took my man from me and I want him back," she said as she stabbed me one last time. Before I lost consciousness, I felt her roughly grab my hand and snatch my wedding ring off. I finally closed my eyes and all the bad shit I had did flashed before my eyes. This was some Karma for your ass. It didn't matter that I had changed for the better. I guess I still needed to pay for my sins. Even if it was at the hands of someone I had never intentionally hurt. As I laid there bleeding profusely, I recited the 23 Psalms over and over again until everything faded to black.

Chapter Fifteen-Dro
Deadly Love Triangle

I was ready for the war that was brewing in the streets. Nothing could prepare for the war that was brewing on the home front. Despite being so in love with Khia, I was also still dealing my ex heavy. When I first came back into contact with Khia, I was no longer with my ex. While I was locked up, we decided to go our separate ways. Once I got released, I started going over and spending time with my kids. One thing led to another and I found myself laying pipe to her every time. I never anticipated falling for Khia or marrying her for that matter. At the time it felt like the right thing to do. Don't get me wrong; I loved Khia and Khiandre as if he was my own.

I was in love with Khia, but I still loved Keshauna and I was torn between the two. Keshauna was my first everything and Khia was my new beginning. I hated that I had been cheating on Khia with Keshauna because she didn't deserve that. I knew that once she found out I was still messing with Keshauna, I was a dead man walking. My scar had just healed from her slicing my ass. I promised her that it was over with Keshauna.

It seemed like since then, I had been spending more and more time with her and my kids and less time with Khia and Khiandre. Khia never nagged, but I knew she was aware that something was going on. I couldn't wrap my mind around how I couldn't let go of Keshauna. In my heart, I knew that I wanted to be with Khia. I just hated to not be with my kids every day. I was tired of how Keshauna made it a habit to hold my kids over my head. Ever since she found out I got married, she had been on straight bullshit with me. Threatening to tell Khia about us and threatening me with Child Support.

I had to buy this bitch a house and an Audi to shut her the fuck up. It was then I knew I had to stop fucking with Keshauna. All she kept doing was throwing up all that she sacrificed for me. Her ass was starting to sound like a fucking broken record.

I was so mad when Khia let that foul shit come out of my mouth. How could she say fuck my kids? That shit really hurt me because my kids were my everything. I hoped and prayed she was speaking out of anger. It would be over if she really felt like that. Khia didn't know, but I had already been thinking about bringing the kids over to meet her.

I left the crib and went straight over to Keshauna's crib. I had to break things off with her. I would just deal with Khia finding out later. I told Keshauna that we were done and that I would be getting my kids every weekend. She started spazzing out talking about how she was going to kill me and Khia and take my kids away from me. Her ass charged towards me and I had to smack the bitch around a couple of times. I wasn't ready to go home, so I headed over and fucked with Malik and Sarge. I ended up getting drunk and I fell asleep on the couch in Malik's basement.

*****

"Dro, get up my nigga! We need to get to the hospital ASAP. Something happened to Khia." I was half sleep, but I was wide awake when he mentioned Khia. I hurried up and handled my hygiene and we were out of the door and in the car. I could tell some shit was serious because the car was quiet except the sounds of Barbie crying.

"Please somebody tell me something!" I was beginning to panic not knowing what the fuck was going on.

"We really don't know what happened to her, Bro. Tahari went to the house to check on her and found her passed out in the doorway," Malik said as he continued to keep his eyes on the road. I knew there was more to it than that. Not long after we arrived, I rushed to into the emergency department. The whole family was already there. Quaadir and Keesha was there as well. I guess the nigga really was a part of the family now.

"Oh, my God! Dro, she was so bloody. Who would do that to her?" Tahari was crying and I was trying my best to hold her up. My mind began to wonder and Keshauna popped in my mind. I almost lost my balance, but I was caught by Malik and Thug. As soon as I sat down in the chair, the doctor came out.

"Is the family of Sha'Khia Davis present?"

"Yeah, I'm her husband and this is our family." My heart was beating so fast and I had a bad feeling in my stomach that he was about to tell me some shit I wasn't ready to hear.

"I have to be straight up with you guys. She lost a tremendous amount of blood. If Mrs. Davis makes it through the night, it will be a miracle. Whoever attacked her really did some damage. A piece of the blade was still inside of her when she was brought in. During her surgery, we found so many injuries to the intestines, but we repaired what we could. She lost her gall bladder due to the severe injury to it. We didn't close her up because she still needs surgery on her intestines. Also, I'm sorry, Sir, but the baby didn't make it. There was just too much trauma for the baby to survive. Right now she can't have visitors. We need to at least get her stabilized. I'll keep you all updated on her condition."

"Thanks Doc," that was all I could say. I was in complete shock. I didn't even know that she was pregnant with my seed. "She has to make it y'all. I fucked up. This shit is all my fucking fault." I had to sit down on the fucking floor to gather myself.

"What the fuck is you talking about, Dro?" Tahari asked as she stood over me.

"I think my Baby momma did this shit to her."

"Where that hoe live at?" Barbie said.

"This shit don't make no sense. It's bad enough her fucking arm was broke in two places. Now, she back there fighting for her fucking life." Thug had to grab Tahari because she was starting to spazz out.

"How the hell did she break her arm?" I had to ask because I wasn't aware that her arm was even broke.

"I took her to the hospital last night. That's how I ended up with Khiandre. She couldn't keep him because she was in so much pain." It was then it donned on me that I had pushed her causing her to fall. I didn't even know she fell that hard. I felt even more fucked up knowing that I had broke her fucking arm. I prayed that God let her pull through. I couldn't live with myself if she checked out.

My phone started to ring and it was this stupid bitch Keshauna. Talking about come and get my kids because she was about to kill herself. I could tell this day was about to go from bad to worse. I hollered at my crew and let them know what was up. I needed to head over to this bitch's crib. I could hear my kids in the background screaming and crying.

It took me less than ten minutes to make it over to her crib. My kids were sitting the porch.

"Why are y'all out here in the cold?" I bent down and kissed each of them on the forehead

"Momma told us to sit out here and wait for you," my oldest son said with tears in his eyes. I put all them inside my car and I went inside to find her. I found her inside the bedroom. I startled her and she turned around and aimed her gun at me.

"How could you love her more than you love me? I gave you everything." This bitch looked crazy as hell. The mascara that was running down her face made her look like a fucking maniac.

"Put the gun down, so we can talk about this shit. You know that I love you and I always will. But, I'm married to Khia now. Did you do that to her?"

"Fuck that bitch. I'm tired of talking. Are you going be with her or me?" Tears were streaming from her eyes and I had already caused damage. I wasn't about to lie to her.

"We talked about this, Keshauna. I want to be with Khia."

"Wrong choice." As soon as the words left her mouth so did the bullets. The first two bullets hit me in the chest causing me to spin around. The next bullet had hit me in the back causing me to fall to the floor. The next gunshot rang out and I didn't feel any pain or burning. So, I knew that she had shot herself. I was able to pull out my phone and call 911. All I kept thinking about was Khia and my kids. This just couldn't be my ending. I never thought loving two women would cause such a deadly love triangle.

Chapter Sixteen- Thug
Why I Love You So Much

I had so much shit on my plate and I was trying my best to deal with it. I had to put my street beef to the side for a minute just until I knew Dro and Khia was okay. That was family and it was fucked up how that shit unfolded. It had me thinking about how I'd cheated on Ta-Baby. Any time I fucked another bitch, I never thought about the consequences behind it. Women loved hard and I never meant to play games with any of them, especially this thot ass bitch Yoshi.

I had told this bitch I was not fucking with her ass like that. She was lucky I didn't blow her fucking brains out for pulling that Facebook stunt. To make matters worse, she kept calling and playing on Tahari's phone. She insisted that it wasn't her doing that, but I knew it was her stanking ass. I knew that Tahari was pissed the fuck off about the bitch getting her number from my phone while I was asleep. The scary part about the shit was Tahari hadn't even shown how angry she was. She had been walking around smiling and laughing. That shit had me on edge because I knew my wife was plotting.

"What are you thinking about?" Tahari asked as she sat up in bed and made eye contact with me.

"I just have a lot of shit on my mind," I said as I exhaled loudly.

"What's wrong baby you need your dick sucked or something?" Before I could respond Tahari put her hand inside my boxers and unleashed the beast. The sight of her freshly manicured hands moving up and down my shaft had pre-cum oozing out. She put the tip in her mouth and licked it all up. She slowly took all of me into her mouth. She put both of her hands behind her back and she started to devour my dick. The sound of her slurping and moaning had me on the verge of erupting.

"Damn, I love the shit out of you." I grabbed Tahari's head and began to fuck her throat. In a matter of seconds, I released all my seeds down her throat. She swallowed them all without hesitation. *I need my ass whooped. Out here cheating on my baby when I got the best at home*; I thought to myself. Tahari got up and went to the bathroom to brush her teeth. She was so beautiful to me. I watched her as she climbed back in bed and on top of me.

"You feel a little better," Tahari asked as she grabbed a blunt from the nightstand. All of our kids were gone except Ka'jaiyah and Kahari. They were cry babies and nobody wanted their asses. It was a good thing they were asleep. It was rare that we got a chance to just sit and converse with one another.

Lately, I'd been running the streets making sure my money was good and flowing. I also made time to go and visit with Khia and Dro. Tahari was dealing with the kids and also sitting with Dro and Khia. Tahari was trying to be strong, but it was really killing her knowing there was a possibility that Khia may never wake up.

"I feel a lot better. Thanks to you. Let me ask you something. Why do you love me? I have given you every reason not to even keep fucking with a nigga."

"I love you because you're everything a woman would want in a man. You treat me like I'm the prettiest girl in the world. You've given me the world without me having to ask for it. I love you because despite being a Thug ass nigga you're so affectionate to me when I need you to be. You're the best father in the world. Despite the doggish shit you've done to me, I know my place in your life and in your heart. Last but not least, you could be with any bitch you want to, but you chose me and I still say yes to you today and every day. No matter what, I'll always choose you first." Tahari snuggled up under me and laid her head on my chest.

"Aww you're making a nigga tear up and shit," I said as I kissed her on the forehead.

"Since we're discussing why I love you. Let me ask you the million-dollar question. Why do you love me?"

"I love you because you love me for me. Not for my money or my street status. I love you because no matter what's standing in the way of our happiness, you make sure no one comes between us. When shit is hectic in these streets, you have my back one thousand percent. I love how you loved Ka'Jairea and Ka'Jaire Jr. as if they were your own. You're the best mother to all of our kids. No matter what's going on between us, you love them and for that I love you even more. You're the love of my life and a nigga like me really don't deserve you.

You should be with a corporate nigga like a lawyer or a doctor. But, you chose me. A hustling thug ass nigga that's in the streets more than he is with you. I love that you never complain even though you have every reason to. I've done some fuck up things to you and the fact that you're still here trying to make it work makes want to love you more and more. Last but not least, I love you because no matter how dangerous shit got for us you were standing right beside me. Not once have you tried to make me choose my street life or my family. That shit means a lot to a nigga like me, Ma. I love you more than anything in this world and I'm not going anywhere unless you're with me. I promise I'm done with bullshit."

I could tell Tahari wanted to cry, but she held it in. I meant every word I said. I wanted to go further and tell her some news I'd been wanting to share with her and my family. After I dead these Gianelli motherfuckers, I was out of the game for good. I was handing everything over to Malik. It was time I focused on being a better husband to Tahari and a even better father to my seeds.

Chapter Seventeen-Tahari
Murder On my Mind

It had been a week since the shooting and Dro had finally waken up. We were all happy when we got the call from his nurse, and I knew that Thug was even happier. He could finally breathe a little easier knowing that Dro was okay. On the other hand, I was sad and starting to lose hope. Khia was still in a coma. No matter what she had did to me in the past, I forgave her. She deserved to be happy with her husband and her son.

Dro was now up and caring for four damn kids. It was a good thing his mother had moved in with him to help take care of the kids. Dro was depressed and it was hard looking at him. I was currently pissed off with him because he hadn't been to see Khia. That was probably part of the reason she was not waking up. I believed his presence would bring her out of the coma. I know that she heard us when we talked. I would see her eyelids twitching and she would squeeze my hand when I talked to her. I'm surprised she hadn't woke up just by hearing Barbie and her annoying ass voice. I loved Barbie, but she had no chill.

I had been trying to get Thug to talk to Dro about not going to visit with Khia. As usual, he told me to mind my business. He said Dro needed time to deal with everything. I wasn't buying that shit. I wanted to curse Thug out for even feeding me that bullshit. It made me wonder if something like that happened to me how would he deal with it. I tried to mind my business, but I couldn't hold back any longer. Today was the day I would make a visit to Dro's house. I already knew that Thug was going to curse me out, but I didn't care. Dro needed to stop sulking and man the fuck up.

****

"What the hell took you so long to open the door?" I asked Dro as he stood in the doorway blocking me from entering. He looked crazy as hell and he smelled like a liquor factory. He had on a white tee and a pair of basketball shorts

"What's up, Sis?" Dro stepped to the side and let me in. The house was a complete mess. Khia was a neat freak, so I knew she would have a fit. I just took my jacket off and started cleaning.

"Where are the kids, Dro?"

"My mother took them out to get some air." He was sitting on the couch looking at the TV. I watched as he turned up the Remy bottle. There were numerous pill bottles on the coffee table.

"Dro, I don't think you should be drinking and taking that medicine. Your wounds haven't healed all the way. You need to take better care of yourself. Khia is going to need you when she wakes up." I took the bottle from him and poured it down the kitchen sink and I returned and sat down next to him on the couch.

"What I'm I going to do if she don't wake up?" Dro put his head down in his hands I knew he was shedding tears.

"That's actually why I came over here. Dro, you have to get up to that hospital and let her know that you're there. She needs to hear your voice. She's responding to me and the other girls. Sitting in this house feeling sorry for yourself is not going to change what happened. Those kids need you more than anything right now. Get it together for your family. I'll finishing cleaning the house. You go get ready to go sit with your wife. Dro headed towards the back of the house and went to the kitchen. At the same time, someone started to beat on the door. I ran into the hallway and Dro was standing there with his gun out to his side.

"Shhh!" He put his finger up telling me to be quiet. I walked over towards him and he swung open the door. I couldn't believe Nico's mother Lisette was standing on Khia's doorstep. She looked just like Nico's ass. I stayed hidden from her because I didn't want her to see me. From where I was standing, I was able to see her though. She was clean and had picked up a lot of weight. I hated to admit it, but the bitch looked good.

"May I help you with something?" Dro asked as he eased his gun into the back of his waistline.

"As a matter fact you can't help me with shit. I'm here to see that lying bitch Khia. She was supposed to be at court yesterday and she never showed her face. I'm sick and tired of her keeping my grandson from me. I hear you think that you're his father. Let me enlighten you, his father is Nicario "Nico" Douglass."

"I'm his father. Now get the fuck off my property before I send you where ever the fuck your bitch ass son is at." Dro slammed the door in her face never giving her a chance to respond. On the other side of the door, Lisette was screaming at the top of her lungs. Telling the whole block how the people in this house had something to do with the disappearance of Nico.

"This shit ain't good for business, Dro. We have to do something about her ass. She's reckless and her running off at the mouth could be our downfall. You had nothing to do with Nico's disappearance, but the rest of us do. I'm not about to do time for killing his bitch ass. Fuck that shit."

"What we going to do, Ta-Baby?" Dro asked he continued to peek out of the curtains to see if Lisette was still out there. It had gotten quiet, so we knew the bitch had finally left.

"I'm a holler at Thug. All I want you to do is focus on Khia. I'll let you know what Thug says."

After discussing the matter for another twenty minutes, we went our separate ways. My mind was all over the place. That bitch Lisette had me nervous. The way she was running off at the mouth at Dro's place, I knew she had been running off at the mouth about Nico to whoever would listen.

****

"Hey Baby. Can I talk to you for a minute?" Thug was inside his man cave watching the Bears game with all of our sons. He loved to watch the game with them. It was their bonding time.

"Of course, we can talk. Let me take the boys to the movie theater and cut on something for them to watch." I sat on the couch and I started to bite on my bottom lip. I was nervous as hell. I know for a fact Thug was going to snap the fuck out when I told him what I wanted to do.

"What's up Wifey? Come here and give me a kiss?" Thug pulled me into his arms and we kissed each other with so much passion. I wanted to beat around the bush, but I decided against it. I was just going to put it all out there on the table. I would deal with his backlash afterwards.

"I want to kill Nico's mother Lisette."

"Come again. Why is that nigga even being mentioned in my presence? He is a dead ass issue, Tahari. Let's leave it that way. Please don't bring this shit up. It's bad enough I have the police all of a sudden questioning me about that fuck nigga."

"Baby, you're missing the point. I'm not trying to bring him up. His mother showed up and Dro's house today. She acted a fool and she started yelling all loud and shit outside about us killing Nico. Baby, you have to let me off her ass. If we don't kill her, she's going to be our downfall. I bet she's the reason why the police was questioning us about Nico and Detective Grimes in the first place." Thug was now pacing back and forth. He did that when he was mad and thinking real hard about shit.

"What the fuck were you doing over at Dro's?" My big mouth ass had forgotten just that fast that he told me not to go over there and to mind my business.

"I'm sorry, Thug. I just had to go over there and talk to him about Khia."

"You're so fucking hardheaded. I distinctly told you to mind your business." Thug was so mad at me, but I didn't care. I wanted to pop off and tell his ass he wasn't my father, but right now wasn't the time to be brave.

"Damn! I said I was sorry. Can I kill Lisette or no?" I didn't come in here to argue and fight with his ass.

"No. Let me and the crew handle the bitch. I don't want you to be a part of any bullshit. Do you hear me, Tahari? Leave the shit alone for now. I need to deal with this Gianelli beef first." Thug was staring my ass down letting me know he meant business.

"Okay." I looked at my husband and lied to him with a straight fucking face. In my heart, I knew that I had to kill the bitch Lisette. I had every intention on murking that bitch sooner than later.

Chapter Eighteen-Barbie
Brokenhearted Reality

Being married to Malik had been everything I dreamed it would be. He came home at a decent hour, he spent as much time with me and Londyn as he could, and our sex life was off the chain. We made love to one another at least twice a day. I couldn't even remember the last time we had an argument. I had no reasons to believe that he had reverted back to his old ways. That was until today when he left his cell phone in our bed while he took a shower.

The buzzing of the phone woke me up. I looked around and I grabbed it. I noticed he had over ten missed calls and even more unread messages. I haven't been through his phone in a long time. Knowing that he hadn't been cheating on me, I didn't have a reason to snoop through his phone. As I held the phone, a text came through. I knew his lock code; it was our daughter's birthday. I entered the code and I clicked on the message. When I read it, I wished that I had never opened it. There was no name to the contact so only the number showed.

(773)547-0096: Lil Malik wants to know can you come to his football game today at 1pm. Call me and let me know if you can make it. The game is going to be at Garfield Park.

As I read the text, my heart started to hurt like I was going to have a heart attack. I felt so sick. I felt vomit rise up in my throat, but nothing came all the way up. The sound of the Malik turned the water off made me hurry up and put his phone back down. The tears were falling from my eyes, but I had to hurry up and wipe them away.

I pulled the covers back over me and turned over so that I wasn't facing him. If I looked him in the eyes, I knew that I would burst in tears. I couldn't believe this shit. I had no clue this nigga had a son on me. I felt him lay in the bed next to me. The sound of him opening his phone made my heart started to beat so fast. I knew he was reading the message. I turned over in bed and now I facing him. He quickly replied and closed his phone.

"Good Morning, Beautiful," Malik said as he kissed my lips. I wanted to fuck his ass straight up, but I had to hold my composure.

"Good Morning. What you got going on today? I was thinking we could take Londyn to Sweet and Sassy to get her nails and feet did. Later we can go out to Red Lobster to eat."

"I have an appointment with the realtor for our new house. You go ahead and take baby girl to get pampered. We can meet up at Red Lobster later." He kissed me on the forehead and started to get dressed. It pained my heart that he said fuck our daughter, so that he could go and be with his son. I wondered did his family know about the little boy. I couldn't believe he already had a son. A namesake at that. Every wife wanted to have her husband's first son. Last month we both agreed that I would stop taking my birth control pills, so that I could get pregnant and give him a son. I laid in bed and watched as he got dressed, before I finally got up and got my daughter dressed.

"I'm about to head out Bae. I'll hit you when I'm on my way to Red Lobster." Malik leaned down to kiss me and I grabbed the back of his head and slipped me tongue in his mouth. I kissed him deeply because I wanted to feel his lips and tongue for the last time.

"Damn Barbie, you kissing me like I'm going off to do a bid or some shit. I love you baby," Malik said as he kissed me and Londyn before heading out the door. I hurried up and threw on a pair of Nike stretch pants and a hoodie. I pulled my hair back into a ponytail and I stared in the mirror as I applied a light coating of makeup. Once I was satisfied with the way I looked, I went into Malik's closet and opened his safe. I took a couple of stacks of money. I didn't have to count it, I just took the shit. I had no plans on returning.

I left the house with nothing that I owned besides the clothes on my back. I grabbed my keys and my daughter. We drove straight to the football game. I needed to see the little boy and his mother. I needed the proof in front of me. After years of his constant cheating, bringing home diseases, and his blatant disrespect for me, I was officially done with his ass. Having a baby on me was icing on the cake. Londyn shouldn't have to share her Daddy with a little boy that

I didn't give birth to. I was so selfish when it came to Malik that I wanted him all to myself. I deserved to have him to myself. I'd held him down since I was fifteen years old.

Damn near the whole relationship I had shared him with some random bitch with the exception of the last year and a half. As I pulled into the parking lot, I spotted Malik's black on black Audi. My blood started boiling and I was ready to tear some shit up, but I had to remain cool, calm, and collective. I had my daughter with me and I didn't want her to see me kill her daddy with my bare hands. I got out and headed towards the football field. I could hear Malik cheering the little boy on as he scored a touchdown.

My eyes made contact with the female standing beside him. I had to blink to make sure I was looking at the bitch Diamond he had cheated on me with numerous times. She must liked getting her ass whooped because I tagged that ass every time I saw her. I was crushed as I watched them interact. He always acted like she was just a fuck. From where I was standing, she was way more than that. I had no intentions on coming here and acting an ass, but all that shit went out the window when I saw that bitch.

Chapter Nineteen- Malik

You Never Miss A Good Thing Until It's Gone

I hated to lie to Barbie this morning. However, I knew that if she ever found out I had a five-year-old son our marriage would be over. I used to fuck with Diamond real hard a couple of years back. When Barbie caught me with her at the club, all hell broke loose. She beat me and Diamond's ass. Barbie went crazy. She busted all my windows out and put my tires on a flat and set all my clothes on fire. The crazy part about it was she burnt all my shit on Diamond's doorstep.

I had to tell Diamond it was over in front of Barbie in order for her to take me back. Plus, I felt sorry for Diamond. Barbie beat the girl's ass every time she saw her. I still crept with Diamond from time to time. It was something about Diamond that I just couldn't resist. I had the total package at home, but being the nigga that I was back then, I continued to cheat. One day Diamond told me that she was pregnant and I told her ass to dead that shit. I couldn't risk Barbie finding out she was pregnant by me. I gave her money for an abortion and the bitch skipped town.

When I never heard from her again, I assumed she was lying about the pregnancy just to get some money out of my ass. Six months ago, this bitch popped up on the block with the little boy. It took everything inside of me not to slap the shit out this bitch. Her ass was a distant fucking memory. Now here she was getting ready to wreak havoc on my marriage. To my surprise, she just wanted me to know that we had a son together.

She assured me that she wanted nothing from me. All she wanted was for her son to know his father. She didn't even have to say anything because I knew he was mine. He looked exactly like my daughter and me. He definitely was a Kenneth. No one in my family knew about him. I had to prepare myself to tell my wife about Lil' Malik. Lately, she'd been talking about giving me a son, so I knew it was going to crush her knowing that I already had a son and he was my namesake. Every time I got ready to tell Barbie about him, I chickened out. I knew that sooner or later, I would have to tell her. Nothing prepared me for how soon that time would come.

"Aren't we one big happy family?" Barbie said as she came and stood beside me. I hated that Londyn was with her. I was shocked as hell. How the fuck did she know I was here?

"What the fuck are you doing here, Barbie?" I regretted coming at her reckless because she slapped me so hard she knocked my shades of my face. It took everything in me not to beat her ass. All eyes were on us and we were drawing a crowd. "Bring your ass on!" I grabbed her by the arm and tried to pull her away from the football field. Our daughter was now crying and I hated for her to see this shit. I picked Londyn up and tried to stop her from crying.

"Let me go, Malik. I want to talk this bitch about her bastard ass child!" Barbie attempted to walk towards Diamond but I stopped her.

"We're not doing this shit here, Barbie." I said through gritted teeth. I looked over at Diamond and I knew that she was scared shitless.

"Daddy did you see my touchdown!" Lil Malik said as ran over and hugged me.

"Yeah, Lil Man. I saw you do your thing." He took his helmet off and all of sudden Barbie stopped ranting and raving and just stared at him. I saw her eyes get glossy. I felt like shit at that moment. Diamond grabbed Lil Malik and she hurriedly walked away with him. She was in no mood to get her ass whooped today.

"What the fuck you running for scary ass bitch? I would like to let everyone out here know that bitch right there fucked my husband and had a baby by him. She's a hoe ladies, so watch your husbands. She's a home wrecking bitch!" This shit was worse than being caught by the TV show Cheaters. All of the parents were staring at us.

I hated that Barbie did this in front of the kids that were out there. I saw the coaches walking towards us, so I forcefully grabbed her and pushed her towards the parking a lot. Once we made it to the parking lot, she started fighting and kicking me. I was trying my best to block the blows. In the midst of us tussling, my daughter had got knocked to the ground and was now screaming and hollering. My reflexes made me slap fire out of Barbie's ass. It made her lose her balance and she fell to the ground.

"You're a stupid ass bitch! Out here performing like this in front of my fucking daughter." I lifted my daughter up and she had cut the inside of her hand open on the gravel.

"You're so damn right. I'm stupid over your black ass. I can't do this shit no more. I'm tired, Malik. I've taken everything you've done to me over the years in stride. Lord knows I fought for this relationship. I've forgiven you every time even when I knew you were still cheating I took you back." I lifted Barbie off the ground and sat her on the hood of my car next to my daughter.

"I know baby and I'm sorry. Let's go home so I can tell you everything. I promise I haven't cheated on you since the last time. A nigga's been on the straight and narrow. I found out about him six months ago. I didn't know how to tell you. Come on Barbie you have to believe me." I held her chin up, so that I could look her in the eyes.

"We've been planning on having a son and giving him your name. You played me, Malik. Why would you give me false hope and make promises you couldn't keep. That shit is wrong on so many levels. My heart is broken right now and you're the cause of it again. He looks just like you and I can't spend the rest of my life looking at him. He will be a constant reminder of your deceit. I want out of this marriage." Barbie took her wedding ring off and threw it at me. She grabbed Londyn and started walking away. I heard her crying and sniffling. That made me start shedding tears like a motherfucker.

"Come on, Barbie. Don't leave like this. Please let me explain." She never even looked back or said a word. She got inside her car and sped away. At that moment, I totally understood the saying you don't miss a good thing until it was gone. She wasn't gone a good minute and I felt like it had been forever. I didn't know what to do. There was only one person that I could talk to and that was Thug. I knew my mother was going to spazz out on my ass when she found this shit out.

Chapter Twenty-Thug
Up In Flames

The sound of the smoke detectors going off throughout the house caused me to jump up from my sleep. I looked around the room and smoke was coming in underneath the door.

"Oh, shit! Tahari, wake up! I think the house is on fire." I was shaking the shit out of her because she was knocked the hell out.

"Oh, my God! My babies, Thug, please get my kids!" We both jumped out of bed and opened the door the hallway was filled up with smoke and we could barely see in front of us. Tahari was crying so badly and that caused her not to focus. If we were going to get our kids out of here alive, we needed to be focused.

"Stop panicking, Tahari, and focus. We have to get the kids out of here." The sound of the kids crying made me rush to their bedrooms with Tahari right on my heels. We made it to Ka'Jairea's room first and that was where all the kids were huddled in the corner coughing and choking. It looked like they tried to come out of the room, but the smoke was too intense.

"Come on babies. Momma and Daddy got y'all," Tahari said as we gathered the kids and exited the room as fast as we could.

As soon as we made it downstairs, the sound of glass breaking let us know that the fire department was there. Our security company had alerted them. The firemen came into the house and grabbed us.

"Is there anyone else in the house?" the fireman asked. We both shook our head no. When we made it outside, I noticed that our kitchen was engulfed in flames; it was a miracle it hadn't yet spread to other parts of the house. I was pissed the fuck off because I knew someone deliberately started that shit. It hurt my heart as my kids and my wife had to receive oxygen due to smoke inhalation. Once again bitch ass niggas felt the need to violate where the fuck I laid my head. This time this shit was more personal for me. My fucking kids could have died in that fucking house.

"Baby, who would set our house on fire?" Tahari cried as she wrapped her arms around my neck. I just hugged her back and held her because once again I really had no idea where it had come from.

"The kids are all fine, but we're going to take them to the hospital to get them checked out just to be on the safe side," the female paramedic said as she got ready to take them to the hospital.

"I'll meet you at the hospital. I need to stay here and talk with the Fire Marshall. I'm going to grab all of us some items and get a suite for us to stay in."

"Please hurry up, Ka'Jaire," Tahari said as she kissed me.

Once I spoke with the Fire Marshall, he confirmed that it was indeed arson. As much as I loved this house, I knew that I couldn't bring my family back there. Their lives meant more to me than anything in this world. I had a pretty good idea that the Gianelli Crime Family was behind the shit, but I didn't have any concrete evidence. I had every intention of getting to the bottom of the shit. I had put my beef with The Gianelli's on the backburner due to the issues with the family, but now I was moving full speed ahead at getting at them motherfuckers.

I put my crew up on what had happened and I wanted them to meet me at the warehouse later on the next day. First, I had to make sure my wife and kids were straight and out of harm's way.

****

"What if we never would have woke up?" Tahari said as she laid her head on my chest.

"Don't even think like that. We all made it out safe and sound. Tomorrow I'm meeting up with the crew to see if we can find out who the fuck is behind the bullshit. I'm sorry we didn't go to a hotel, but my momma insisted that we come and stay here with her. With Vinny still being out of town she's a little lonely.

"It's okay baby. I actually feel safe here with her. I called Marta to let her know what had happened and she had a fit. She told me she was ending her vacation early. She should be here sometime tomorrow."

"I miss Marta. She's the best."

"I do too, but we have to continue doing what we're doing as far as the kids go. I don't want to put our kids off on her. We have to raise our own kids."

"I totally agree baby. Get you some rest I'm going to go check on the kids." All the kids were asleep except for Ka'Jairea. She was sitting up in the bed watching Frozen. That was her favorite movie and she would watch it over and over.

"What's up babygirl? You should be sleeping." I laid in bed next to her. She looked just like my sister, but I was starting to see features of Kelis in her. It was hard for me to look at her sometimes, especially since I had offed that bitch.

"I can't sleep, Daddy. I'm scared that lady is going to try and hurt us again." She sounded like she was about to cry.

"What lady baby girl?" I took the remote out of her hand and cut the TV off.

"The lady that was in our house. I heard Ka'Jaiyah crying, so I got up to check on her. When I went in her room, the lady had a pillow over her face. I asked her who she was and she said that she was a friend of you and Mommy's. She told me not to tell you that she was there because it was a surprise and that y'all couldn't know. After that, she left. I got my sister and the twins and took them into my room. I woke up Ka'Jaire and told him to come in my room with us. That's when I smelled the smoke. I was so scared Daddy. I'm sorry I didn't tell you and Mommy sooner. Are you mad at me?"

"Of course not. I'm proud of you Baby girl. You saved your sisters and brothers. You're such a good big sister. I'm going to take you to the mall later and buy you something really nice."

"Just me and you right? I don't want Ka'Jaiyah to go, she will cry all day." I held back my laughter because none of the kids wanted to be bothered with her. She was so bossy and territorial when it came to her Daddy.

"Just us. I need you to promise me that you won't tell Mommy about the lady being in the house. It has to be our little secret."

"I promise, Daddy." She hugged me and turned the TV back on. I was livid because I knew the only bitch that overstepped her boundaries was that hoe Yoshi. All week she had been throwing shots on Facebook and threatening me on my voicemail. That bitch just signed her Death Certificate. I couldn't believe this bitch was getting ready to smother my fucking daughter. I couldn't let Tahari know that she was behind it or I would never hear the end of it. I wanted to kill that bitch myself. Just when I thought shit couldn't get worse, it did.

Chapter Twenty-One- Tahari
Bitches and More Bullshit

I couldn't believe what I overheard my daughter and Thug talking about as I headed to the bathroom. I hated that I had to eavesdrop on their conversation. When I heard my daughter say that the bitch put a pillow over my baby's face all I had was murder on my fucking mind. How could Thug even think that it was okay to keep some shit like that from me? I forgot all about having to use the bathroom. I went right back in the room and laid down in the bed. He wasn't even ready for the tongue lashing I was about to give his ass.

"I thought you was sleep."

"So, your bitch tried to kill us, huh?" Thug was looking like a deer in headlights as I stared his ass down.

"What are you talking about, Ta-Baby?" he asked with the goofiest look on his face. I wanted to slap the shit out of him for trying to play on my fucking intelligence.

"Don't fucking play with me, Ka'Jaire Kenneth. I heard what Baby girl told you. What pisses me off is the fact that you told her not to tell me. Let me find out you trying to protect that sideline hoe. I will shoot you in more than your ass this time around. I play many fucking games, but when it comes to my kids I will kill a bitch dead."

"Calm down and lower your voice. I don't want to wake my kids or my mother up," Thug said as he sat down on the side of the bed.

"Please don't tell me to calm down. Are you fucking serious right now? I don't have a calm bone in my fucking body. It's your fault why this shit happened anyway. It's always some bullshit with these psychotic ass bitches you be fucking. If you learned how to keep your dick in your pants we wouldn't have to go through all these fucking changes."

"Pipe the fuck down, Tahari, and watch your mouth! I can't believe that you would blame me for some shit like this. You know I would never intentionally put you or my kids in harm's way. That's real fucked up that you would let some shit like that come out your mouth."

"I'll tell you what's fucked up nigga, you keeping this shit from me. It's cool though because I'm going to handle that bitch myself. If I wait for you to do some shit we'll all be dead."

"I wasn't going to keep it from you, Ta-Baby. I just wanted to check the shit out first. You know I don't act on impulse. If I did, we wouldn't still have our freedom or our lives."

"Whatever, Thug, I'm not trying to hear that whack shit you saying." I watched as Thug balled his fist up and clenched his jaws. He started to rub his temples like he was trying to calm down. He jumped up from the bed and got in my face.

"I see why that nigga Nico used to beat your ass. You talk too fucking much. No matter what the situation is you just keep talking and talking. Shut the fuck up sometimes. I really don't appreciate the shit that you're saying to me. Your ass lucky I don't be laying hands on your ass because I would have been reached out and popped you in the mouth."

"I can't believe you would say some fucked up shit liked that to me." That shit really hurt that he would throw Nico up in my face like that. The ass whoopings I received from him was something I hated to even think about. For Thug to say he would pop me in my mouth had me on the verge of tears.

"You can't believe I would say some shit like that, yet you talking reckless about me. Like I'm not a good ass nigga or I can't protect my fucking family. Not once did I bring up how your crazy ass mother and father was shooting my fucking house up and you running around here fucking a nigga that was gunning for me. I could say my life has been hell since I met your ass and the only good thing that came out of it was my kids, but that shit wouldn't be right because I love your ass."

"You don't love me, Thug. Fuck this shit. The only good thing that came out of it was our kids and we gone keep it that way;

strictly Baby Momma and Baby Daddy going forward. You can believe that shit."

I laid down in the bed and pulled the covers up over me. I turned my back to his ass. I refused to cry because he said what he said. It hurt my feelings, but I had to admit we both said things to each other that we shouldn't have said. He basically said this relationship wasn't shit. He probably didn't mean it, but there was certain shit that you couldn't take back once it was said. I was not about to fight or argue with him anymore.

I was going to show him better than I could tell him. If our kids were the only good thing that came out of our relationship then that was the only level we needed to be on. Fuck that husband and wife shit. I'm going to show his black ass better than I can tell him.

The next morning, I got up and got dressed. I had received a call from Dro saying that Khia had finally woke up from her coma. I needed to go see her and then go to the Doubletree Hotel and check on Barbie. She was crying so hard I could barely understand what she was saying to me.

"Thanks, Momma Peaches, for keeping the kids for me. I'll be back as soon as I can." I kissed each one of my kids on the forehead. I past right by Thug's ass.

"No, kiss for your husband."

"What husband? Last I heard nothing good came out of this, but our kids. See you later Baby Daddy."

"Both of y'all really need to stop this childish ass shit," Peaches said as she put her cigarette out in the ashtray. I kept walking towards the door. I wasn't trying to hear shit. I said what I said and I meant it.

Thug was blowing my phone up and texting me. I didn't answer or respond to his text. I had better shit to do besides hear him talk shit to me. I knew that he was pissed off about me calling him Baby Daddy. I couldn't help but laugh as I pictured his face in my head when I called him that. He was gon' learn today.

Once I arrived at the hospital, I went inside the gift shop to get Khia some Get Well balloons and some flowers. As I rode the elevator, all I could do was think about how I was going to kill the bitch Yoshi. I wasn't going to hide from Thug or sneak and do it behind his back. I just refused to wait for him to handle it.

****

"Hey Boo. I'm so happy that you're awake. How are you feeling?" I said as I walked into Khia's room and kissed her on the forehead. I noticed that she was just staring off into space and her eyes looked glossy like she was about to cry. "Khia, talk to me. What's wrong?"

"I'm so fucking mad at Dro right now. I don't even want to see or hear his ass." Khia wiped the tears from her face that had fallen.

"Don't be like that, Khia. He has really been going through it since all this shit happened. He almost lost his life as well. That crazy ass baby momma of his better be lucky she killed her damn self because I would have killed her myself."

"What are you talking about, Tahari?" Me and my big ass mouth. Dro hadn't told her about all of the events that had unfolded while she was in coma.

"Nothing. Don't worry about it. Let's just focus on you getting better and coming home to Khiandre." The look on Khia's face let me know that she wasn't buying the way I tried to cover up my tracks. For the rest of the visit, I caught Khia up on all the other shit that was going on within the family. It was imperative I let her in on my plans with Lisette.

After giving it much thought, I knew that she needed to handle that bitch with my help of course. It was good to see Khia get up and walk around. Her doctor said that her stomach was healing just fine. It was a miracle she didn't have to wear a colostomy bag. During the whole visit, I could tell that Khia's mind was a million miles away. This shit had really traumatized her. Hopefully when she was released from the hospital she would get better. Dro was going to need for her to be in her right state of mind because they now had four kids to raise.

After visiting with Khia, I made sure to call Dro. I told him that he needed to tell Khia about the shit that went down with his Baby Momma. Once I handled that, I headed over to the Double Tree Hotel to meet up with Barbie. I didn't know what the hell was going on with her and Malik. The way she was crying on the phone I knew that the shit wasn't good at all.

I sent her a text and she gave me her room information. When I arrived, she opened the door and she looked a hot mess. Entering the room, I sat down on the bed with Londyn and watched her as she combed her American Girl Doll's hair. Barbie was sitting in a chair by the window staring out of it. I could tell that she was in deep thought. I wanted to ask her what was wrong, but I just decided to wait it out until she was ready to talk.

While I waited, I got up and started cleaning the room. There were potato chip and candy wrappers everywhere. Not to mention, the numerous amount of old bags of takeout. The room was a hot mess. I looked over at Barbie and she was smoking a cigarette and that was a shocker because I never knew that she smoked.

"Malik has a five year old son. I went through his phone and that's how I found out. I saw the little boy and he is the splitting image of Londyn and Malik. I can't believe this shit, Tahari. All the shit I have put up with from him. We haven't even been married a year and it's over already." Barbie was crying so hard that she had me crying. Since I met her, she had rarely shown any emotion behind Malik's bullshit. So, to see her in such a fucked up state had me hurting for her.

"Are you serious? Do you know who the bitch is he has a baby by?"

"Yeah. He used to fuck with her a couple of years back. I caught them together and he promised me the shit was over. He claims he didn't know about Lil Malik until about six months ago. He carried this shit around all this time. He straight played my stupid ass. This nigga had me thinking we were working on giving him a namesake and he knew that he already had one. I have been nothing but good to Malik. Why does he continue to hurt me like this?" Barbie cried on my shoulder and I just held her. I was speechless because I really didn't know what to say. I just wanted to console her.

"What do you plan on doing, Barbie? We both know that you can't stay up in this hotel forever. Get your stuff, we can go over to Momma Peaches' house. That's where Thug and me are since that crazy bitch Yoshi broke in our house last night and tried to kill us."

"Are you fucking serious? I know that bitch is not still breathing?"

"Her ass won't be breathing for long. I got something for that hoe."

"I'm not going to Momma Peaches' house. If I go there Malik will come and try to talk me out of getting a divorce. Plus, I don't even want to see his deceitful, lying ass face. Don't tell Momma Peaches either she will try and contact me. The last thing I want to hear is that Malik getting molested is what causes him to do the foul shit he does. That excuse has ran the fuck out."

"You can go stay at my old house. No one will think to find you out there. Thug doesn't even know I still have that house. It's paid in full. I just make sure I pay all the bills every month. I promise I won't tell anybody you're there. You can stay there as long as you want."

"Okay, but you have to let me pay you rent." Barbie got up and started gathering all her belongings, which wasn't much.

"You don't have to pay me anything, Barbie. We're a family, remember? Let's just hit the mall up and go grocery shopping. I can't have you feeding my niece all this damn restaurant food." We both laughed and checked out of the hotel.

For a brief moment, I was able to get Barbie to laugh. Once we finished shopping and I dropped her off, she was right back to being sad. I helped her get settled in and I gave her my set of keys. I was so worried about her. Knowing that she was in safe environment with Londyn made me feel one hundred percent better.

As I headed to my next destination I couldn't help but to shake my head at the bullshit Thug, Malik, Dro, and Sarge put us through. Their asses needed to get it together and stop engaging in all of this foolishness. They're married men with children. It was time they started acting like it before it was too late.

****

It had been two hours since I had been sitting outside of Gentleman's Paradise waiting for the bitch Yoshi to come out. I needed to keep a low profile because the last thing I needed was for Markese to see me and tell Thug on my ass. He was already pissed off at me because I hadn't answered for him all day. I had already hit Trish up and she told me her schedule. I told her what was up and made her promise not to tell Markese. The pyromaniac ass bitch should be leaving out of the club at any minute now.

About twenty minutes later, I observed the bitch leaving the club. I was surprised to see her leaving out of the side entrance of the club. I had to do a double take just to make sure my eyes weren't deceiving me. Yoshi was not alone; she was with Quaadir.

Everything inside of told me to call Keesha on his sneaky ass, but curiosity got the best of me.

As soon as he pulled off, I followed his ass. I stayed far behind him so that he wouldn't notice someone following him. The route he was taking was all so familiar to me. It was the route we took to get to the warehouse. Quaadir pulled into the warehouse and that was when I saw Thug's Bugatti parked in his parking spot. Those sneaky motherfuckers was trying to kill that bitch without me. Thug knew what I was on all this time.

I watched as Quaadir pulled Yoshi out of the car and threw her over his shoulder. He must have drugged her ass because she was conscious and all smiles when she walked out of the club. I sat in my car and waited a couple of minutes before I went inside. If Thug thought he was going to kill that bitch without me he was sadly mistaken. She tried to hurt my babies and that was the ultimate no-no. It was time for me to join the party and I gave less than a fuck about not being invited.

Chapter Twenty-Two- Thug
Taking Out The Trash

I had thought long and hard about everything Tahari had said
during our argument. I agree with her in regards to me telling Baby
girl to keep it a secret from her mother. That should have been
something I told her immediately. I was trying to be deceitful by not
telling her. I knew if she knew she would go out and do the very
thing she was doing now. My wife thought that she was so slick with
her sexy ass. But, she forgot I taught her everything she knew. Our
argument didn't have to go as far as it did. She actually escalated the
argument so that she could come out and be on some bullshit. In her
frame of mind, she was thinking if we were into it then I wouldn't
bother her or try to keep tabs on her. I was onto her ass the minute
she walked out the door with that whack ass Baby Daddy shit.

Unbeknownst to Tahari, I was ten steps ahead of her. When she
went to sleep, I hit Quaadir up and told him I needed his help with
some shit. He had already been busy linking back up with the
Gianelli Family, so that we could take their asses down. Quaadir had

proven to be beneficial to the team. I know a lot of people wanted me to kill his ass, but he was no use to me dead. If I would have killed him, I would still be out here fighting a war against motherfuckers I never even knew. Tahari and Keesha were a lot alike; as soon as Quaadir ran the plan down to her, she started with the jazzy mouth and the questions. All I could do was shake my head as I heard them arguing as if I wasn't even on the phone.

The plan was simple. I knew that Yoshi was weak for a nigga with fat pockets. I couldn't send in Sarge, Dro, or Malik. She knew their faces, so Quaadir was my only choice. Once the bitch saw him in V.I.P making it rain on the other hoes, she would be on his dick without hesitation. I had already put Markese up on game. I had him cut off all the security cameras inside and around the establishment before Quaadir could even make it so that there would be no traces of him ever being there. Once inside, he would get close to Yoshi and get her to leave the club with him. I knew that thirsty, money hungry bitch would beat him out the door.

****

"Wake up bitch!" I said as I slapped the shit out of her to wake her up. Blood dripped from her lips and fell down her chin. She began to stir around, but was unable to move because she was tied to a chair.

"What the fuck did you do to me nigga?" she said as she stared at Quaadir who was leaned back while smoking a blunt.

"Don't worry about it bitch. Save your strength, you're going to need it."

"So y'all was gone start this party without me. I didn't get an invite or nothing. I'm pissed off because I should have been the one throwing this motherfucker." The sound of Tahari's voice and her Christian Louboutin's clicking across the cement floor caused us all to shift our attention to her. My wife was looking sexy as hell in a black leather jumpsuit with her hair pulled back into a high ponytail. She was on good bullshit. I looked over at Quaadir just to see if he had any lust in his eyes. If he did, he was doing a good job at hiding it. I didn't give a fuck if we had a truce. If I caught that nigga looking at my wife I would put a fucking bullet in his head without hesitation. Yeah, I could admit I was a jealous ass nigga when it came to my Ta-Baby.

"What the fuck are you doing here, Ta-Baby? I was gon' call you. Damn, let me handle shit." All I could do was shake my head as she pulled some black leather gloves from her back pocket. At this point, I knew there was no talking to her. I had to let her do her.

"You know what, Tahari, this all you. I'm not going to fight you anymore," I said as I sat down next to Quaadir and started smoking the blunt.

"Her and Keesha ass is definitely sisters. I have to go through this same shit back home," Quaadir whispered to me. We both laughed and got ready to watch Tahari perform. Her ass was in rare form and nothing good would come out of this.

"You love my man dick so much that you wanted to smother my fucking daughter!" Tahari started raining down blows on Yoshi. The sound of her nose cracking made me cringe. "This shit don't feel good do it?" Tahari had taken her hands and covered Yoshi's nose and mouth causing her to damn near turn blue.

"Fuck you, your kids, and your husband!" Yoshi managed to say as she tried to catch her breath.

"Shut the fuck up!" Tahari said as she drop kicked her and made her fall over in the chair and onto the floor.

"Don't sit there Baby Daddy. Go and get the gasoline, so I can burn this bitch alive. She likes to play with fire, so I'm going to let this bitch burn. I'm not about to waste another minute on this hoe ass bitch. Let me ask you something ,Yoshi, a bullet in your chest wasn't enough to keep you away from my husband. That was some good ass dick, huh?" Yoshi was crying and sobbing, but that didn't help her at all. I grabbed the gasoline and handed it over to her. I watched as she started to douse Yoshi with the gasoline.

"See bitch your first mistake was fucking with my kids. Don't get shit twisted, this ain't about no dick. The collapsed lung I gave your ass was punishment enough for fucking with my husband in the first place. Fucking with Ka'Jaire Jr., Ka'Jairea, Kaine, Kash, Ka'Jaiyah, Kaia, and Kahari is a death sentence off top. See you in hell bitch!" Tahari lit the match and threw it in her. Her ass lit up instantly.

Tahari just stood there looking at her like it was nothing. I had seen her in action before, but her killing Yoshi was different. Her rage had escalated and I better had got my shit together before she fucked around and kill me. She had a nigga shook.

"Thanks for grabbing that bitch, Quaadir. Call the cleanup crew. I'll see you at home." Tahari kissed me passionately on the lips and chucked up the deuces as she walked away. I was speechless, but I followed her directions.

****

When I made it back to my mother's crib, Malik was sitting at the table looking a mess. He was drinking Patron straight from the bottle. He better hoped Peaches didn't come in here and see him drinking her shit. She was gon' snap the fuck out. The last thing I wanted to hear was her mouth about us drinking her shit.

"What's up, Lil Bro?" I said as I grabbed a shot glass and poured a drink.

"Barbie left me for good this time, Big Bro. I fucked up. Remember the bitch Diamond I used to fuck with. This bitch shows up six months ago with a little boy claiming that he's mine. The fucked up thing about it is, he looks exactly like Londyn and me. I didn't know how to tell her man. Some way she found out on her own and she took my daughter. I don't know where she at. The last thing she said to me was that she wanted a divorce."

"Damn nigga that's some deep shit. I know your ass ain't over their crying." I knew my brother loved Barbie's crazy ass, but to see him cry had me feeling bad for him. "Have you tried calling her?"

"Yeah, she's not answering. I tried that where's my Iphone app, but she has her shit cut completely off. I can honestly say I don't know what I'm going to do if she' gone for good."

"You know how Barbie is. She's in her feelings right now. Just give her some time to come around. I'll ask Ta-Baby have she talked to her. Look, I'm about to go upstairs and lay down in Ma bed until she gets here. I need to talk her about what to do."

"Where she at anyway?"

"She went out to dinner with Vinny. He just made it back in town a couple of hours ago." Malik went upstairs and I went upstairs to see what my wife was doing. I couldn't help but think of Vinny. Lately, I'd been having an eerie feeling. Some shit was definitely not right with this nigga. He had been gone damn near a month to Miami. During this time, he rarely contacted us.

Peaches would say that she talked to him, but it seemed like he had been dodging me. That was fine by me because I didn't trust his ass these days. I hadn't told anyone how I felt. My mother was in love with his ass and the last thing I wanted to do was rain on her parade. Peaches deserved some happiness for a change. On everything I loved, if that nigga playing games with my mother, I was going to kill his ass.

As I walked inside the bedroom, Tahari was sitting up reading her Kindle. I found myself just staring at her in amazement. Not even three hours ago, she tortured and killed someone. Now she was sitting up in bed Indian Style looking beautiful as ever. Without a care in the world.

"Why are you staring at me like that?"

"Because you're so beautiful." I walked over and took the Kindle out of her hand and pushed her back on the bed.

"Oh no! Get your ass back. The best thing that came out of this relationship was our kids, so you don't need none of this good pussy." Tahari tried to push me away, but I pinned her down and put all of my body weight on her.

"Stop being like that. We both said things to each other that we shouldn't have said. You know you're the best thing that ever happened to me. I don't know where I would be without you. You're the mother of my children and I love you more and more every day. Even though your ass is crazy." I placed kisses all over her face and they neck

"I love you too. You really hurt my feelings when you said that, Thug."

"I'm so sorry. Let me make it up to you." I pulled her panties off and opened her legs as far as they could go. For a minute, I took in the beauty of her pretty pink pussy. She had the type of pussy that made a nigga's mouth water just from the sight of it. Neatly shaven and always had the freshest smell. I took my time sucking on her inner thighs and slowly made my way up to the promise land. I sucked on her swollen clit. I could feel it throbbing on the tip of my tongue. I went in for the kill and I started to devour her pussy like it was my last meal on this Earth. I found myself moaning out in pleasure as I made love to her with my tongue. Tahari was trying her best to get out of my clutches, but I held on to her tight.

"Thug, I'm about to cummmm!!

"Yeah, that's right cum for Daddy." On command, Tahari started squirting releasing her juices all over my face and in mouth. She had the bed soaking wet. I stood up and took off my clothes. Tahari crawled towards me and massaged up and down my shaft. Her hands alone had a nigga ready to erupt. She licked all over my head catching all the pre-cum. Without hesitation, she placed my entire dick in her mouth. I could feel my shit touching her tonsils. Slowly and methodically she bobbed up and down as she massaged my balls. I grabbed the back of her head and pushed it down farther

"Mmmm! Suck your dick just like that." My eyes rolled in the back of my head as I felt my load shoot straight down her throat. She caught it all of course.

"Turn that ass around. I'm not finished with that pussy yet." I smacked Tahari on both of her ass cheeks as hard as I could.

"I love it when you smack my ass like that baby!"

"Oh, you do." I roughly entered her and started pounding the pussy and smacking her ass at the same time. I was all up in her guts and I was trying fuck the soul out of her. I was showing her ass no mercy as I hit her G-spot over and over again.

"Ahhhhhhhhh! Oh, my God! Please don't stop, Thug."

"You like how I give you this Thug Passion?"

"Yesss! I love this Thug Passion. I'm about to cum all over this dick.

"Well cum then, so we can cum together." We both came simultaneously. Tahari fell flat on her stomach and I laid on her back with my dick still inside of her.

"That was the shit baby!" Tahari said out of breath.

Before I could respond, the sound of Malik busting inside the room door caused both of us to jump and grab the covers.

"What the fuck Lil Bro?"

"I'm sorry y'all, but we have to ride out. Ma just called me and said to come and get her. She said something didn't feel right to her. I hit the niggas from the block and told them to meet us up there."

"I'm about to fuck this nigga up if anything happens to her!" I jumped up and put my clothes back on.

"I'm coming ,too," Tahari said as got up and started getting dressed.

"Call Keesha to come and sit with you until we get back. Please just listen and don't fight me on this."

"Okay I'll stay, but make sure you call me and let me know y'all are okay." I leaned down and kissed her and was out the door. My mind was all over the place. Peaches was my heart and soul and a hair better not be out of fucking place.

Chapter Twenty-Three- Peaches
Love The Way You Lie

The entire time that Vinny had been gone I longed for him. All I wanted was for him to come home. At one point things were all good. It seemed like after we got married he became a different person. It was odd to me that he just jumped up and had to go to Miami all of a sudden. He told me that it was for business, but for him to be gone a whole month had me questioning some shit. I knew some shit had to be going on.

As a husband and the father of my children, he was supposed to get here quick fast in a hurry when I told him about the Quaadir situation. As we talked on the phone, he acted as if he wasn't concerned. He barely even said a word. I thought that he would be anxious to meet Quaadir, but he acted nonchalant about the whole situation.

A lot of crazy shit had been happening lately. I felt like I was constantly being followed. A couple of times someone had put dead fishes wrapped in newspaper on my doorstep. I didn't know who the fuck was playing games with me, but for some reason in my heart I knew that it probably had to do with Vinny's ass. Leaving those fishes on my doorstep was some Italian shit that meant swimming with the fishes or death. In a nutshell, I didn't know what the fuck was going on, but I had pretty good idea Vinny's ass did. I decided not to tell my kids what was going on. Mainly because they were already in war and they needed to be focused.

I was glad when Vinny called me and said that he was back in Chicago. He wanted me to meet him at his restaurant and I didn't understand why he just didn't come home to our house. It was him who purchased me this big ass house and he had hardly even lived in it. Once I made it the restaurant, I was so happy when I saw him. The look on his face let me know that he wasn't as enthused.

"Hey Baby. I missed you so much," I said as I wrapped my arms around his neck. He gave me a dry ass hug.

"Hello my Bella. How are my kids and grandchildren?"

"How about you call them and find out?" I couldn't believe he was asking me that shit when he wasn't even staying in contact with them. I watched as he gestured for the waiter to come and he brought wine to the table.

"Why are we here, Vinny? I would much rather us be at home spending quality time with each other."

"I have some important things to discuss with you."He never even looked me in my face. He just continued to sip on his wine. I was getting real irritated at his demeanor and the way he was acting. Not to mention, he kept looking around like he was nervous or something. I scanned the room and that was when I realized there wasn't a lot of people in the restaurant. I noticed that there was men spread out in the restaurant. Maybe it was nerves, but something wasn't right. That made me nervous, so I excused myself and I went to the bathroom.

While in the bathroom, I called my sons. Thug didn't answer, so I talked to Malik and told him to come to the restaurant. When I headed back to the table, I observed Vinny talking on his phone.

"Is everything okay, Bella," he asked as he kissed me on the cheek.

"I'm fine. Let's get out of here I'm not feeling too well."

Before he could respond, the sound of gunfire erupted inside of the restaurant. I felt wetness on my face when I looked over at Vinny and his fucking head was gone. I was in shock and I couldn't even scream. I started to feel pain and that was when I felt my stomach. Blood was pouring from it. There was more gunfire and that was when I saw some of Thug's workers exchanging gunfire with the Italian men that were sitting in the restaurant prior to me going to the bathroom.

"Come on, Ms.Peaches, we have to get out of here." The guy I knew as King picked me up and carried me outside. When we made it outside, I watched as Quaadir, Thug, Malik, Dro, and Sarge continued to exchange gunfire. I was starting to lose consciousness, but not before I saw Malik got hit by some bullets. The pain from the wound in my stomach was nothing compared to the pain in my heart I felt seeing my son get shot. That alone made me pass out and everything fade to black.

Chapter Twenty-Four-Barbie
Never Want To Be Without You

I had been absolutely miserable without Malik. As much as I hated his fucking guts right now. I missed and loved him so much. I hated that I'd been keeping Londyn away from him. No matter what he loved her so much and she loved him. It didn't help that she was constantly asking for him. That makes this even harder for me. I've been crying non-stop over this. I have no appetite. I couldn't sleep for shit. I hated that this has happened to us.

I felt like all that I had been through with Malik that I deserved my happily ever after. How could he lay next to me in bed and make love to me knowing he was keeping a secret that had the potential to hurt me? I never wanted to be without Malik, but I couldn't be with him behind this shit. Not only did this shit hurt, but it was also embarrassing. He was giving all these bitches out here in these streets a reason to laugh at my ass. Especially that bitch Diamond. I wish I knew where she lived because I would go and whoop her ass.

"Is Daddy that little boy's Daddy?" Londyn climbed up in bed with me. I wasn't sure how to answer her question, but I needed to tell her the truth.

"Yes. Baby he's his Daddy, too." The tears fell from my eyes as I said it. The realization had really settled in.

"It's okay Mommy. Don't cry. Daddy still loves us." Londyn kissed me on the jaw and it made me cry even more. In my heart, I wanted to believe that he still loved me. If this was his way of showing his love he could keep the shit. I had become nauseous so I had to run to the bathroom and I vomited everywhere. Nothing was really coming up but liquid because I hadn't eaten anything. My head was hurting so bad that all I wanted to do was sleep.

I managed to get up off the floor and crawl in bed. I put the TV on Nickelodeon for Londyn so that I could sleep without her interrupting me. I had just closed my eyes when someone started banging on the front door. It scared the shit out of me because no one knew I was here, but Tahari. I heard her calling my name, so I jumped out of bed and answered the door.

"Go put on some clothes. We have to get to the hospital." The look on her face let me know that it was something wrong with Malik.

"Oh, my God! What happened?" I had to sit down on the floor because I felt like I would pass out. Tahari pulled me up and hugged me real tight.

"I don't know what happened. Thug called and said Peaches and Malik got shot. Vinny was killed."

I had to let everything she said sink in. I threw on a jogging suit and gym shoes and got Londyn dressed. I dropped her off to Marta and we headed to the hospital. I prayed that God brought both of them out of this. I hated Malik for having a baby on me. However, I didn't hate him to the point that I wanted him dead. The entire ride to the hospital was quiet. We were both deep in our own thoughts. I dreaded going inside the hospital.

"Come on, Barbie. We have to go inside."

"What if he's dead?" I put my head down in my hands and cried.

"We're not claiming that. Malik is strong and right now he needs you more than anything. Plus, Momma Peaches needs us. She has been here for us though everything. Come on Sis they need us." I wiped my face and followed Tahari inside of the hospital. We went to the Emergency department and we were ushered into the family room. As soon as I walked in, Thug and Ta'Jay rushed over to me and hugged me so tight. I became dizzy and I started throwing up again. I almost passed out, but Thug caught me before I could hit the floor.

"Go get a doctor!" Some people rushed in and place me on a stretcher and took me to a room and they hooked me up to machines and started running tests. Before I knew it, I was completely out of it.

I didn't know how long I had been out of it. When I came to, Tahari was asleep in a chair next to my bed. I sat up in bed and I still had a massive headache. I started unhooking all of the machines and that made them beep like crazy. I didn't give a fuck though I needed to find out what was going on with Malik and Peaches. The beeping sounds woke Tahari up and she rushed towards me.

"Where the hell are you going? You scared the shit out of us. The doctor said he wants to keep you because you're severely dehydrated and it's not good for the baby."

"Baby?" I was confused because I had no idea I was pregnant. On the other hand I wasn't surprised because prior to our fallout we had been fucking like rabbits.

"The doctor said that you are five weeks. You need to take better care of yourself." Tahari was always trying to be a mother figure. Right now I wasn't trying to hear shit. I wanted to know if my fucking husband was going to be around to raise this baby.

"I understand all that, but I need to know what's going on with Malik."

"Malik is still in surgery they're trying to remove a bullet that's lodged in his back. As for Momma Peaches she is going to be okay. The family is still downstairs waiting."

"Well come on, I want to be with my family." I was scared as hell for Malik. I wish that we wasn't fighting when he got shot. I probably wouldn't feel so bad. I really felt like shit right now. It was a must that he made it through this. I couldn't even imagine living life without him.

****

"The family of Malik Kenneth." The sound the doctor's deep voice caused all of us to jump towards our feet. "I know that his mother is in recovery, so I need to speak to the next of kin."

"I'm his wife and these are his brothers and sister." I was trembling as I spoke. Thug grabbed my hand. I could feel how nervous he was as well. I just knew he was about to tell me something that I wasn't going to be able to handle.

"Mr. Kenneth is a lucky man. He was shot in the head, but the bullet was stuck in his skull. It never penetrated the cerebrum. He sustained a gunshot wound to the chest that caused both of his lungs to collapse. We had to insert a tube inside his chest so that he could breathe. A bullet hit him in the Femur and shattered it. We were able to repair, but he is going to need physical therapy in order to regain full use of it again. We were unable to move the bullet in his back and it's just too risky to move it. So, far now we will just leave it. It's not close to the spinal cord right now. In the event that it starts to shift. The bullet will have to be removed immediately."

"Can we go see him, please?"

"Not tonight, he needs a lot of rest. I think it will be better if everyone comes back tomorrow. He needs to rest."

"Thank you so much," I said as he shook Thug's hand and walked away. All I could do was breathe a sigh of relief and shed a couple of tears. They were happy tears though. God had answered my prayers. We all went back to Momma Peaches' house. Everybody was really quiet. I guess everyone was taking in the night's events.

As soon as we made it to the house, I went straight upstairs to sleep. I wanted the morning to come quick, fast, and in hurry. Some shit must really be brewing because the entire family including Quaadir and Keesha were all here. Not to mention all their goons. Shit was about to get real if King, Dutch, and Nasir were here. Them lil niggas were crazy. Thug and Malik basically raised them and taught them the game. They were some little crazy fuckers. Not to mention Markese, Rahmeek, Killa, and Boogie was in attendance. It was about to be a fucking bloodshed in the Chi.

The next morning came quicker than I thought. I got up and went to our house. I wanted to get me some fresh clothes and grab some of Malik's toiletries. He had sensitive skin and I knew that he would have a fit if I let him put on hospital lotion; he was so damn picky. I grabbed something quick to eat and made my way to the hospital. I retrieved a visitor's pass and I made my way up to his room. When I entered the room, Diamond was sitting on the bed holding his hand. He was wide-awake and his eyes got big as saucers when he looked up and saw me.

"Really bitch. I have the right mind to beat your ass right now. I can't believe you, Malik. I have been going crazy ever since I heard you got shot. Crying my eyes out and your ass in here playing house with your Baby Momma. I'm so over this shit."

"Barbie, it's not what you think. There is nothing going on with Malik and me. I was already in the hospital. I heard what happened and I just wanted to check on him. I'm leaving right now. I'll bring Lil Malik later." Diamond grabbed her purse and tried to rush out of the room, but I was on her ass this time. She wasn't running away from the conversation this time. I hurried up and caught her on the elevator.

"You're getting a kick out of ruining my family, aren't you?"

"In the past I wanted nothing more than to ruin your family. Malik was the first nigga that ever treated me good. He cut off what we had because he was too afraid to lose you. I left it at that. I moved to Iowa after I found out I was pregnant. I told Malik and he gave me money to get an abortion. At that point, all I had was my unborn child. I didn't want to cause problems in his life, so I took his money and kept my secret to myself." The elevator door opened and she rushed off the elevator and went into the bathroom. I continued to follow her.

"If that was the case, why didn't you stay away? How could you just show up out of the blue?" She was really starting to piss me off by acting all nonchalant and shit like she wasn't fucking up my family. It was taking everything inside of me not to slap the shit out of her.

"I came back because I'm dying. Eight months ago, I found out that I have stage four Breast Cancer. I have less than six months to live. I don't have any family. I just wanted my son to be with his father when I died. I didn't want my baby in the system. Please Barbie take care of him. It's not his fault; please don't punish him because you hate me. Malik doesn't even know that I'm sick. I was about to tell him when you came in the room I just came from the doctor and I was getting everything in order for when I go on

Hospice. He wants to admit me into the hospital because he thinks I have Pneumonia," Diamond cried uncontrollably and I felt like shit. Regardless of me wanting to beat her ass, I knew that she needed us. I didn't know what I would do if I had to leave Londyn.

"Stop crying. We'll take care of him. Come on let's go back upstairs. You need to tell Malik what's going on." I gave her some tissues for her face.

"I don't feel too good. Please tell him for me. I need to find Lil Malik a baby sitter while I'm in the hospital."

"Go get him and bring him back. I'll keep him while you're in the hospital." I couldn't believe I had just said that shit. I could be a bitch, but I was not a heartless bitch.

"Thanks, Barbie. I promise I'll be right back with him." She gave me a hug and left out the washroom. I had to gather myself before I went back up to Malik's room. Regardless of how I felt about Diamond, I really felt sorry for her and her son. I loved my husband and I knew that he would want me to accept his son. It was going to be hard at first, but eventually I'd get over it. I needed to get some pointers from Tahari because she was the pro at raising kids that weren't hers. When I walked back into Malik's room, he was fully dressed and ready to go.

"Where the hell are you going?"

"Get me the fuck out of here ,it's not safe. Thug already moved Peaches. Don't ask any questions let's just go home."

"Here are your discharge papers and prescriptions for some pain medicine and antibiotics, Mr. Kenneth. I really do not agree with this. You're in no condition to be up and out in the air," the doctor said as he handed him the papers.

"I'm good, Doc. My wife will take care of everything." Just like that, we were leaving the hospital and headed home. On the way, I told him everything that Diamond had told me about her illness. He called Diamond and we went and picked Lil Malik up. Diamond went and admitted herself into the hospital. We also stopped by Marta's and grabbed Londyn. Malik insisted we stop and get her. He was struggling to breathe and that was scaring the shit out of me.

"Are you sure this is a good idea, Malik. Baby, you don't look too good." I rubbed his forehead and he was burning up.

"I'm going to be okay, Barbie. Just get me home. The family is coming over to stay with us for a couple of days. We all need to be together right now. Thug doesn't want us to be separated."It's a good thing we had an eight-bedroom house, five bathrooms, and a full basement. I wanted everybody to be comfortable. When we made it home, I got Malik situated so that he could get some rest. I gave Lil Malik and Londyn a bath so they could also relax.

"My mommy is really sick. She said that you're going to be my new mommy. Is that true."

"Diamond will always be your mommy. I'm just going to help Daddy take really good care of you. You and Londyn are brother and sister. You have so many cousins. I can't wait for you to meet them."

"Londyn said that Grandma Peaches is the best grandma in the world. I never had a grandma." I just stared at him; it was so freaky looking at him because he was the splitting of Malik. I would definitely have to get used to having him around.

Later that night, we all laid in bed with Malik and we watched TV.

"Be careful. Don't hit Daddy's leg." They were wrestling and if they hit that leg, Malik was going to shit bricks.

"They're cool. I like seeing them get to know each other. Thanks for taking this shit in stride. On the outside, you're putting on a smile to please me. I know that this shit is really hurting you on the inside. I'm so fucking sorry for all of this. I never meant to hurt you, Barbie. You have to believe me. I have not cheated on you since a little bit before making this shit official. I love you so much and I can't risk losing you behind no bullshit."

"Shhh! We believe you." I took his hand and placed it on my stomach.

"You bullshittin'." I shook my head no and I leaned over and kissed him. I loved this man with all my heart. He was not perfect, but he was perfect for me. It was crazy how one minute I hated him and the next minute I felt like I was going to lose my mind if I had to live without him. I guess this that shit Nivea was singing about in her song *Complicated.*

Chapter Twenty-Five- Thug
The Bloodshed Begins

The thought of someone hurting my mother and brother had me livid. All I wanted was blood. These bitch ass Italians really had me fucked up. There was definitely some shit not sitting right with me and the first thing was why Vinny's own people would kill him. Despite him helping me out in my time of need, for some reason him being dead didn't faze me not even a little bit.

I'd been a street nigga for a long time and something told me he knew that shit was coming. Peaches was fucked up behind seeing his fucking head being blown off. I really wanted to talk to her about what happened prior to the shooting. There was a reason why she called us to come to the restaurant. When we pulled up, there already was a shootout between the fucking Italians and my young niggas King, Dutch, and Nasir. They were laying them pasta-eating motherfuckers down. I felt like a proud parent.

I taught them how to lay a nigga down without hesitation. It was a good thing they made it the restaurant or Peaches would have been dead as well. It was a miracle King was able to still buss his guns while carrying my mother without him or her getting hit. That nigga was a beast.

Malik was my world and seeing him get shot in front of me had a nigga shedding tears. Since he was little boy, I'd made it my job to protect him. If he would have checked out I don't know where I would be. I loved my family with everything inside of me, and it was starting to become too much. I hated that people were trying to hurt not only me, but the people I loved the most.

My decision to leave the game was becoming more concrete. I couldn't keep putting my family in these dangerous situations. Before I leave the game alone, I intended on laying a lot of motherfuckers down. I was not going out like a bitch ass nigga. When I left this shit alone, I was going to be a fucking legend. Regardless to my street credit, I lived for the fact that my family looked up to me. I couldn't take them getting hurt; it was like I was not protecting my family.

I hadn't had a wink of sleep since the shooting. I needed to get some rest because the next morning we had to get an early start to get everybody all moved to Malik's estate. They lived out in the boondocks further from the city than us. Our wives were dead set against us sending them out of town.

I was kind of skeptical about Malik checking himself out of the hospital. He was adamant about getting out of there, so I moved

Peaches immediately. She was already at Malik's house resting comfortably. She made it clear that she didn't want to be bothered with anyone. However, that shit couldn't fly. I made sure to tell Barbie to check in on her anyway. As soon as I made it to Malik's tomorrow, her and me needed to talk. I really didn't care if she was not in the mood. I needed to know what happened.

I was so tired when I climbed in bed with Tahari that I didn't even take off of my clothes. Before I could fall all the way asleep, I felt her get out of bed and come around to my side. She peeled my shirt off of me. Next, she untied my strings on my Timberlands and pulled them off of my feet. Finally, she unzipped my pants and pulled them off.

Tahari had the softest most gentle touch. She sent electric currents through my body with the slightest touch of her fingers. I wasn't expecting what she did next. She put her hand inside the slit of my boxers and gently massaged my shaft. I let out a slight moan. She pulled my boxers down to get better access to what belonged to her. The tense feeling I once had was now replaced with peace and relaxation as she made love to my dick with her mouth.

I was hardly ever rendered speechless, but for some reason this time it was different. I can feel my toes curling and hands gripping the sheets. Tahari was talking to my dick with her tongue as she glided it up and down my shaft. The sounds of her gagging and slurping had me releasing sooner than I wanted. After draining me, she went to the bathroom to freshen up. Not long after, she came and climbed in bed with me. She curled up under me and held me tight like I was going somewhere.

"Do you feel better?"

"I'm good, Ta-Baby." I kissed her on her forehead as I rubbed my fingers through her hair.

"You are not good. I know you, Thug, and all of the shit that's going on is starting to take a toll on you. Baby, you have to understand that you can't control everything. Some things are just beyond your control. Since the day I met you, I've watched you take care of everybody. That's one of the things I admire so much about you. You're so selfless. You put everybody and their needs in front of you and yours. I need you to understand that it's okay to take care of you and let someone else be in control.

"I'm the head of this family and I have to be in control at all times." I didn't mean to cut her off I just had to remind her of my status.

"I know that, Ka'Jaire. I guess what I'm trying to say is it's okay to let someone take care of you. You need someone to go hard for you as well. That's why whenever shit gets hectic. I don't mind setting it off for you. I apologize if sometimes I overstep my boundaries when it comes down to getting in your business. Baby, I just want you to sit back, relax, and let me kill people that bring harm to us. You've been protecting me since the day we met. Let me protect you in return. I know that the shit that's going on with the family is overwhelming. I know that you feel bad about Peaches and Malik getting shot, but baby it is not your fault. Trust and believe me, they don't blame you at all." Tahari was now sitting up in bed looking into my eyes as she spoke to me.

"You know your man so well, huh?"

"I'm your wife, best friend, mother of your children, and your Bonnie. It's my job to know you and understand you. Since we've been together, I have learned more about you than you think I know. I just keep it to myself for times like this. When you're overwhelmed, I will always be here to relieve your stress. No matter the method that I use to do it."

"I love you so fucking much." I pulled her on top of me and guided myself into her wet opening.

"I love you too baby. I'm here for you no matter what." Tahari sucked on my fingers as she slowly rode my dick. I felt myself all up in her guts touching the spot that had become all so familiar to me. I just wanted to sleep, eat, live, and breathe in the pussy. It was just that damn good. Tahari took me to another place as I rode her waves of ecstasy. Not long after, we were spent and laying in bed basking in the glory of one another. In the morning, it would all be over because I was ready to set it the fuck off and kill any and everything in my way.

****

The family had finally made it to Malik's house and everyone was situated. It was a good thing Malik had a guesthouse. Marta insisted that she would stay out there with all of the kids. Dro's mother, Helen, was also staying in the guesthouse with her helping with the kids. Khia still needed help getting around, so I thought it would be a good idea for her to come since she took care of Khia. I hired nurses to come in and make sure that they were well taken care of around the clock. Everyone was in the house except Tahari and Keesha. They went out to Wal-Mart to shop for items we would need while staying at the house. In the meantime, it was time to talk to Peaches before we had the meeting with the crew.

I walked in the room and she was sitting up while Barbie was trying to feed her some soup.

"Come on, Momma Peaches. You haven't eaten in two days. Come on please eat something before you make yourself sick."

"For the thousandth time, I'm not hungry. Please just leave me alone." Peaches pushed the tray away and continued to stare off into space. Barbie threw her hands up in defeat and shook her head as she walked out of the room. She gave me a look that said good luck.

"Hey, Momma. How are you feeling?" I kissed her on the forehead and sat on the bed beside her.

"I'm fine, Ka'Jaire. What do you want?"

"I want to know what happened when you met up with Vinny. Something freaked you out and that's why you called me and Malik."

"The only thing I can remember is how Vinny was acting all nervous and shit. He was constantly looking over his shoulders. I looked around and there were a couple of Italian guys in suits. They were spread out in the restaurant. Something didn't feel right, so that's when I went to the bathroom and called you guys. I wasn't even back at the table a good minute before the shooting started. The man who I saw shoot Vinny was the damn waiter. I can't believe I'm a widow. This shit unbelievable."

I hugged my mother as she cried herself to sleep in my arms. I felt sorry that she had to go through this because she really loved Vinny. I had to sit back and observe some shit that maybe the rest of the family didn't pay attention to. Vinny was the Boss of the Santerelli Crime Family. It was one of the biggest Mob Families in the World.

Vinny came back into our lives unexpectedly and all of a sudden he wanted to be in our lives. The fucked up thing about it was that we were never apart of his world. Yeah, he called himself giving me Miami, but that shit came with a cost. We almost lost our freedom. Vinny knew damn well the FEDS were on to him. We all left Miami and he did also.

He put on a good ass front for my mother and he had me convinced to a certain extent. That was until he hopped his ass back on a fuckin plane to Miami. If the FEDS were building a case against him down there, why in the fuck would he go down there to conduct business? That should have been the last place he wanted to go to.

When we came back to Chicago, we were never introduced to his family as his children or my mother as his wife. We were still his black shame and I was over the shit. He couldn't be in our lives publicly when we were growing up, so I don't know what ever made us think that he would be in our loves publicly while we we're grown.

My mother called and told him about Quaadir and you would think the nigga would at least want to meet his long lost son, but he acted as if he didn't have a care in the world. I let that man come into my world and be around my family. We were nothing but a pawn in his little game.

Since my mother was resting, I needed to head to Malik's room and put our plan to action. Walking into the room, I observed our usual crew. I had King, Nasir, and Dutch in attendance; the way they handled themselves had me wanting them to move up in the ranks. They had no idea of the big plans I had.

"I'm sorry I took so long. I needed to sit with Peaches. Let's get down to it. What do we have on these motherfuckers that violated us?"

"I know for a fact one of the shooters was Dominic Gianelli and he's the grandson of Don Gianelli. The one who hired me. The rest were also Gianelli associates. I've seen them from time to time when we've had business meetings. Since I've been well I've had surveillance on their estate. It's been the typical coming and goings, but lately I've observed his daughter Donatella frequenting the estate and that's surprising because she lives in Miami with her husband and children. Her son happens to be Dominic Gianelli," Quaadir said

"There has to be a connection between the Santerelli's and the Gianelli's. If we figure that out we'll find out where this shit is coming from," Malik said as he winced in pain.

"We kept an eye on Momma Peaches house all night and there was nothing strange or out of place. Before I pulled off to come here,

I saw the mailman put this big package on the doorstep. I didn't want to leave it out there, so I waited until he pulled away and I grabbed it. It's a good thing I did. Look at who it's from and who it's addressed to," King said as he handed me a medium sized brown box. It was addressed to Peaches from Vinny.

"Nigga make sure that shit ain't ticking or nothing," Sarge said as he moved back in fear of the box. We all laughed at his big coward ass. I did however put it up to my ear to listen just to be on the safe side. I decided to open it and see what was inside. I did it carefully and skillfully. Inside of the box was a DVD and a lot of papers. There were instructions also that told my mother to look at the DVD first and then go over the paperwork that was included. At first I was going to watch the DVD without my mother, but whatever the contents were, she needed to see them herself.

"Go grab Peaches, Quaadir. She needs to see what's on this DVD." Minutes later, he ushered her into the room. He guided her over to the bed and she laid next to Malik. The pain meds had him in and out of it.

"What the hell is going and why is there a box with my name on it? Wait a minute I know you motherfuckers didn't open my mail. It's already bad that y'all some damn killers and drug traffickers, but now y'all into mail fraud now. You punk ass niggas do know that that is a federal offense." She tried rising up, but the pain her stomach wouldn't let her.

"Calm down, Momma Peaches. You're going to bust your stitches with all that hollering," Dro said as he went over to sit her back down.

"Vinny sent you this in the mail." I handed the instructions and she had a confused look on her face. Her eyes were glossy like she wanted to cry, but she held it in.

"Play it. Let's see what it is. I'm dying to know what it could possibly be." King put the DVD in and pressed play. Vinny's face appeared and he began talking to my mother.

"My Dearest Bella, If you're watching this then most likely I'm dead. I hate that things ended this way. I want you to know that I have always loved you since we were teenagers. I loved my kids as well. I just couldn't be in their lives because of who my family was. I'm not going to beat around the bush. There are some things about me that you don't know.

It breaks my heart to know that I have betrayed you, my sons, and my grandchildren. I'll get straight to the point because I have bullshitted you long enough. You and I are not legally married. I've been married to my wife Donatella for many years. We also have two sons together Dominic and Vinny Jr. It was easy to keep both of my families away from each other.

Unfortunately, my wife found out and her father Don Gianelli has a price on not only my head, but also on Thug. Mainly, because he stands to inherit the Santerelli empire. Despite my father's distaste for me having kids with a black woman, he has always had a trust fund set up for not only Thug and Malik, but also Quaadir. I had no idea how he knew about him. Especially, since I had no idea myself.

As the years went by and the boys started to get older, my father took interest in the way Thug ran his organization. That was why he chose to do business with him, so that he could get to know him better. Since my father is dead, my brother Marco is dead, and now I'm gone, our empire goes to the oldest grandchild since Thug was born five minutes before Quaadir he is now Head of the Santerelli Crime family. The papers that I have provided will tell you everything you need to know in regards to the homes, businesses, and territory in which Ka'Jaire now owns.

I know that all of this sounds easy, but it's not. Donatella and her father Don Vito cannot except the fact that Dominic or Vinny Jr. will not inherit the empire. That's why they are doing everything in their power to kill off the bloodline. As you know, they have knocked me off. It's imperative that my sons kill all of them motherfuckers and take their rightful places on the throne in which they deserve.

Bella I have changed my will and you will receive everything that I own. You deserve it for all of the heartbreak that I have caused you. I love you Bella. Tell my sons and my grandchildren that I love them very much. Please follow all the instructions that I have left for you. The world is now yours and my children. I know that this doesn't make up for my deceit. I just hope you find it in your heart to forgive me."

The entire room was quiet as the DVD player stopped. I was speechless at what the fuck I just heard. No wonder this nigga was at my head. I was the Boss of a fucking Mob Family now. Just when I had every intention of getting out of the game, I get thrust right back in. This shit was deeper and on a whole different level. How the fuck I'm I going to tell my wife that her husband is now a Mob Boss? I looked over at my mother and her head were down in her hands.

"Are you cool, Ma?" I got up from where I was sitting and I kneeled in front of her.

"I'm good son. I'll be even better when all them motherfuckers are dead. You and your brothers deserve to run this fucking city and now that it's definitely yours. Y'all need to execute and eliminate the competition. Now if you don't mind, I have a funeral to fuck up." Peaches kissed me on the forehead and walked out of the room like she wasn't in any pain. I had a feeling I was about to get a dose of the gangster Peaches I used to see when I was a shorty.

I couldn't believe this nigga Vinny already had a fucking family. What was his purpose of asking my mother to marry him? That was fucked up. I know that Peaches is heated about that. She could put on that gangster persona all she wanted she was still a woman and I knew she was hurting. In the meantime, I had some big ass decisions to make. I was not even sure I wanted this shit that had been given to me.

I looked around the room and I locked eyes with Malik and Quaadir. I could tell that they were trying to read me and see what I was thinking. I could also see that they wanted this shit bad. Looking over at my right and my left hand nigga's Dro and Sarge, I could tell that they were ready for whatever. Last but not least, I looked over at my protégés King, Nasir, and Dutch they had murder in mind and their trigger fingers were ready to do damage. A knock at the door brought me out of my thoughts.

"Hey Baby. I brought y'all some bottles of Remy and ten Kush blunts. Malik is not to drink or smoke a damn thing." Tahari set everything down and left the room.

"So, what's it going to be, Big Bro?"

"It's about to be a bloodbath and I guess I'm the Boss of what used to be the Santerelli family. We're not riding under that shit. Every nigga in this room is a Thug to his fucking heart. You all have showed and proved your loyalty to me over and over again. I respect you niggas for putting your lives on the line day in and day out for my family and me. Quaadir, I know that you have your own thing popping back in the A, but you're more than welcome to join us at Thug Incorporated. Despite our past differences, you've shown me that you kept shit one hundred with me and I know that you will be a great asset to this empire. You don't have to answer right now. Just let me know."

I popped one of the bottles of Remy open and poured myself a shot. At the same time, I fired up a blunt and let the smoke marinate inside of my lungs before I blew it out.

"I guess a toast is order," I said as I held my glass up high and so did everybody else including Malik. "To Thug Incorporated!"

"To Thug Incorporated!" We all said in unison and knocked back our shots. For the rest of the night, we put our plan in motion to take down the Gianelli's. I was ready to start my reign with no bullshit. Once all of this shit was over, I needed to sit down and map out positions in this family. No one's hard work would go unnoticed.

Chapter Twenty-Six- Peaches
Don't Fuck With My Heart

I should have known that motherfucking Vinny was no good. All the signs were there I just put the shit in the back of my mind. I was pissed because I was cool just fucking him. It was his old ass who threw marriage into the deal. The fact that he had a wife and other kids had me livid. I was not mad because they existed; my issue was the fact that he couldn't tell me that. He approached me when Thug was in trouble after killing his people.

We had several conversations prior to us even taking the shit to the next level. At anytime he could have been a man and told me he was married with children. The shit would not have bothered me one way or another because I had no feelings for him. Just like the Italian snake he had always been, he slithered his way back into my life and wreaked even more havoc. It was one thing to play with my heart, but please don't fuck with my kids or my grandbabies.

I was too fucking old to be in love triangles and shit. I didn't have a problem with putting this Thunder cat on him and sending him on his merry little way. This nigga wanted to start talking love and marriage. I should have known his bitch ass was too fucking good to be true. He lucky they blew his fucking head off because I would have blew his dick off if I would have found this shit out sooner.

I was mad ass fuck because I had a fucking bullet hole in my stomach and my kids were being targeted because of who they were; heirs to the Santerelli Empire. This was some straight bullshit. I already had more fucking money than I knew what to do with, but I would gladly take what the fuck Vinny left me. I deserved that much. That son of a bitch got me hotter than a firecracker on the Fourth of July. It was cool though my kids and me would get the last laugh; we always do.

It had been a week since Vinny got killed and his funeral had finally arrived. The Italian motherfuckers probably wouldn't welcome me, but I gave less than a fuck, I was going to make my presence known. I made sure to have my partner in crime with me; my sister Gail. Her ass was even crazier than me. She had just changed her life and was more laidback. Our son's would kill us if they knew what we were doing. No need to worry because if some shit got funky, I had an arsenal in my Birken bag. We were both dressed to the nines in our red custom made Diane Von Furstenberg two piece pants suits.

As soon as we pulled up to Holy Family Church, I could see that the family was just heading in. I watched as people were holding up what I guess to be was his wife. Bitch bye. Y'all killed the man. His son's followed closely behind and consoled their mother. These people were worse than black folks at a funeral. They were really putting on a show.

"Are we going to sit here and sight see or are we going in? My man get off work at three and I need to be home when he gets there," Gail said as she fixed her makeup in her compact mirror.

"Shut your ass up, Gail. I wanted to wait until they all went inside and were seated. I need to make a grand entrance." We sat there for about twenty more minutes. As soon as we started grabbing our purses, there was a knock at the window. I looked up and I almost shitted bricks. It was Thug and Markese's ass.

"Did you tell them where we were going?" I asked Gail as she looked like a deer in headlights.

"Bitch, you know damn well I didn't say shit. Knowing their asses they probably followed us."

"Roll down the window, Peaches." Thug called me by my name, so I knew that he was upset with me. I rolled the window down, but I wouldn't look at him in his face.

"I'm not mad that you're here. You should have told us so that we can be your escort."

"Please, Ka'Jaire. Get out of here with that bullshit. You never would have let me come." I wiped the tears from my eyes that were threatening to fall.

"I would have let you come because you have the right to be here just like anybody else. That's why we're all here." I stepped out the car and the whole family was in attendance minus the kids, Khia, and Malik. Malik or Khia were in no condition to be outside. I was amazed as I saw Tahari, Barbie, Ta'Jay, Keesha, Aja, Stacy, Nisa, Trish, Quaadir Sarge, Dro, Rahmeek, Boogie, Killa, King, Dutch, and Nasir. They were dressed in all black and looked like they were ready for whatever.

"Look at all these crazy motherfuckers!" Gail said and we both laughed in unison.

"Come on, Ma'. We're going in as a family and leaving out as one as well. Know that if some shit jump off, we are strapped and ready for whatever," Thug said as he opened my door and took my hand. We all walked up to the church and walked in like we owned that motherfucker. All eyes were on us.

The church was huge so it took us a minute to make it to the front. I walked up to the casket and rubbed my hand across the top of it. It looked as if it was fourteen karat gold. It was gorgeous. With everything inside of me, I hawked up the biggest glob of spit and spit on that motherfucker. Fuck him. Yes, I had every intention on spitting on that motherfucker. Too bad he had a closed casket.

"You black bitch! You need to get the fuck out now. How dare you come in here with these black gangbangers and their whores and disrespect my husband?" Before I knew it, I had slapped slob out this bitch's mouth. Gail was right behind me and slapped her ass, too. Security jumped up and had their guns cocked and aimed. They weren't ready for us though. We all had our guns out as well as all of the men and the ladies were ready to let bullets fly and kill all these motherfuckers. I had this Victoria Gotti looking bitch by the collar with a gun at her fucking temple. There was plenty of security, but not enough to fuck with me and mines.

"Fuck you and your husband. Let's get something straight you white ass bitch. These are not gangbangers, as a matter fact, these two are his fucking kids. Not to mention, the head of their father's family. But, you already knew that bitch. Since you and your jealous ass family is the reason why we're here anyway. I'm not mad though bitch. I actually thank you for offing his good for nothing ass. My children and me have inherited every fucking thing he owned. Checkmate Bitch! Let's get the fuck out of here."

"All of you black motherfuckers are dead!" one of her sons said.

"We ready whenever your bitch ass is," Thug said as we all backed out of the church slowly with our guns still aimed and ready to blow. Once outside, we all jumped inside our cars and went back to Malik's house and had big ass party in honor of that fucking rat Vinny being dead. I refused to sit around and cry over spilled milk. I was not going to lie and say that the shit didn't hurt because it did; I had really fallen in love with Vinny's ass.

As I sit here and nursed my cup of Patron and smoke my damn Newport, I couldn't help but think about the mind blowing sex I used to have with Vinny. That Italian motherfucker was hung like a damn horse. Whoever said white men had little dicks was dead ass wrong. Now that I thought about it, that was about all I was going to miss about his snake ass. I couldn't wait until Monday to go to the lawyer and get everything that had been left to me. That bitch Donatella should have crossed her T's and dotted her I's. That bitch would have to live off of Daddy's money because her husband's money was coming straight to Peaches.

Chapter Twenty-Seven-Khia
Nipping Shit In The Bud

Ever since I was released from the hospital, Lisette had constantly been harassing me. The last straw was when this bitch stood outside of my house with a bullhorn telling my neighbors about Nico and the fact that Dro and me had something to do with him being missing. I was glad Dro wasn't home because he said the next time she stepped foot on our property, he was going to kill her ass for trespassing.

The shit with Lisette was really starting to get under his skin. I was tired of her shit and the bitch had to go. I promised Tahari that I would let her help me off Lisette, but this was my problem and I had to deal with it. Not only for me and my son, but for Thug and Tahari as well. It was my time to put in work for them. They had enough shit going on in their life.

My wounds have healed really well, but I was not one hundred percent just yet. Dro had been taking care of me since I was released from the hospital. He felt guilty about what happened to me and he should feel bad. He had no business cheating on me with his Baby Momma and I hoped he learned his lesson.

His kids were not bad kids at all. It had just been hard to connect with them because their mother put shit in their heads about my son and me. I didn't know where I would be without Dro's mother. She had been a really big help with all the kids and I was so happy she has accepted Khiandre as her grandchild. It would hurt my heart if she didn't.

She was real close to his Baby Momma. I still had nightmares of that bitch attacking me and taking my ring off of my finger. When I told Dro that she had took it off my hand, he went out and got me a bigger and better one. I was happy he got me another one, but the one he put on my finger at my wedding was sentimental. That was the ring I wanted. Ain't no telling what that psycho ass bitch did with my shit.

Dro had been all over me. I really just wanted some time to myself. When he wasn't around, he had his mother on security patrol. I was tired of him and her ass watching my every move. I couldn't even go to the bathroom with him standing there with tissue to wipe my ass. I knew that I would get a chance to be by myself when I saw everybody going to Vinny's funeral. Dro's mother was in the guesthouse with the kids and Malik was in his room high off his pain meds as usual.

Once the coast was clear, I threw on an all black jogging suit and a pair of all black Air Force Ones. I checked in my purse to make sure my gun and my silencer was in there. Dro had brought it for me months ago, but I never used it. I wished I had it on me the day his crazy ass Baby Momma stabbed me up.

I was on a strict time schedule. I needed to make it to the city and back in an hour. I had to beat Dro back to the house. I didn't want him knowing that I had been gone. I managed to sneak out without being noticed. I called Lisette and told her that we could meet up so that we could discuss the visitation schedule for Khiandre.

Thirty minutes later, I was pulling up to the new house in which Lisette was now living in. She swung the door open before I could even make it on the porch good.

"Where is, Lil Nico! I thought you were going to bring him?" Lisette was pissed off, but I didn't give a fuck.

"I never said that I was bringing him. I said I wanted to meet up so that we make a schedule for him to come and visit you. Can I please come in?" Lisette stepped to the side and allowed me to enter her house. I sat on the sofa and she sat on the loveseat. We were facing each other.

"Before we can do anything, Khia, I just need to know why did you betray my son? He took care of you and gave you the world. Now you're hanging with Tahari and her King Pin husband. I know they have something to do with Nico's disappearance." Lisette was crying, but that shit didn't faze me. I didn't give a fuck about her or Nico.

"Let's get some shit straight, Lisette. You of all people know how ruthless Nico was. On several occasions, he beat me until I was unconscious. He sometimes would beat me to the point where I couldn't even walk. You need to stop acting liking Nico was a saint. Lisette you know that he was robbing all the local hustlers. You're so adamant that Tahari and her husband had something to do with it, let's keep this shit one hundred, that shit could have came from anywhere."

"Do you even care about what has happened to him?"

"As a matter of fact, I don't. My life has been so much easier without him in it. Wherever he is, I hope he stays there and away from me and Khiandre."

"That's another thing that has me pissed off. How could you change his name? That's his namesake." She was now standing up looking crazy as hell.

"I don't have time for this shit, Lisette." I turned around and acted like I was about to leave, but I was really pulling the gun from the pocket on my hoodie. Before I could even turn back around, she had jumped on me and started attacking me. I was trying my best to get the bitch off of me plus, I didn't want her to hit me in my stomach where I still had staples. We ended up falling on the floor.

When we fell, the gun flew out of my hand. It didn't go real far and was in arms' reach; all I had to do was reach and get it. Lisette's old ass was starting to get tired, so I used that as my advantage to grab the gun. When I was able to grab the gun, I hit her in the face and head with it repeatedly until she was out cold.

Once I stood up and gathered myself, I let off two rounds in her skull. I looked around and made sure I didn't touch anything or that I hadn't stepped in the blood that was now pooling around her head. I used the sleeve off my hoodie and opened the door and did the same thing when I closed the door behind me. Once I was inside my car, I breathed a sigh of relief. I looked at my cell phone and I was good with timing; I had thirty minutes to make it back to the house.

*****

"Hey Baby. How are you feeling?" Dro asked as he came into the room and sat next to me on the bed.

"I'm good. Just ready to get out of this bed and join the rest of the family."

"If you're up to it, get dressed and come out there and kick it with us. I'm so glad you're able to get up now. I couldn't stand the fact that you had to stay confined to a bed all this time. I'm so fucking sorry for everything." He kissed me on my lips and I reciprocated the favor.

"You don't have to keep apologizing, Dro. I survived I'm here. Let's just forget about it." I got up and went into the bathroom and I heard a knock at the room door. It was Dro's mother.

"Where is, Khia? I came in here am hour ago looking for her and she was gone and so was the car. I thought she wasn't able to go to the funeral." See how nosey her ass was. I didn't think about her coming to check on me. I was in the bathroom shitting bricks.

"I thought she wasn't well enough either." I heard the anger in Dro's voice as he spoke. I was nervous as hell.

"Bring your ass in here, Khia!"

"I'll be out in a minute." I was trying to buy some fucking time to think of a lie.

"I'm not going to say it again. Bring your ass here now!"

"What's wrong with you?" I played it off like I didn't know what the hell was going on.

"Where did you go today?" He was now standing right in front of me towering over me. I couldn't even look at him in the face; I was so scared.

"I just went to the store. I needed some air. The walls were starting to close in on me."

"That's lie number one. I advise you to tell me where the fuck you went. I can't believe you're standing here lying to me." I hated that he knew me so fucking well.

"Okay damn. I went to see Lisette." I started biting my lip because I wasn't prepared to tell him what the hell happened although I knew I would have to.

"Really, Khia? I told you do not go to her house alone. Tell me what happened because the look on your face tells me that some shit popped off. Let me sit down to hear this shit." Dro was really being dramatic right now.

"We got into a heated argument. She attacked me, so I shot her in the head twice. Baby please don't be mad at me, I had to do it. Lisette was running off at her mouth too much. It was either her or us. I'm Team us, so that bitch had to go."

"I understand all of that. You're supposed to run shit pass me before you act on it. It's too much going on right now for you to be sneaking your ass out of the house committing murders. What if something would have went wrong? I wouldn't have known shit. Don't you ever do no shit like that again. Do you hear me, Khia?"

"Yes, I hear you. Loud and clear."I got down on my knees in front of him and unzipped his pants. He was mad at me, but he wouldn't be for long. I reached my hand inside his pants and pulled out his pulsating dick. It had been so long since I was able to please him. I was about to enjoy every minute of pleasuring my husband. There was no need for me to take things slow. I went straight in for the kill just the way he taught me. He loved that sloppy toppy head and that was exactly what I gave him.

"You're real sorry, huh?" Dro was fucking my face with so much force that I thought he would injure my damn tonsils. I nodded my head up and down letting him know that I was definitely trying to show him how sorry I was. Not long after, he released in my mouth. I started sucking as if my life depended on it. I wanted to drain him dry.

"Damn. That was the shit Ma," Dro said as he laid back on the bed and fired up a blunt. It had been a minute since I was able to smoke and that shit was smelling good. I gestured for him to pass the blunt, so that I could hit it. I laughed on the inside because it was shame that some good head will make a nigga forget he was just mad at you. I'd been working my magic on him since I was a teenager. I was now his wife and that shit still had him tapping out after all these years.

Chapter Twenty-Eight-Cassie
Bitter Bitch

It never ceased to amaze me how this bitch Peaches managed to hold her head up high. She walked around as if she was the fucking Queen of England. The bitch was nothing but a home wrecking hoe that ruined my life. Peaches took everything from me that I deserved. No matter how many years went by I still hurt from Peaches' betrayal. She acted as if I was the scum of the Earth when her ass was really scum of the Earth.

First, she falls in love with Venom. Next, she gets pregnant by him. Finally, she gets her hooks in not only Ta'Jay but Keesha as well. This bitch had turned my daughters against me. They were all I had left in this world. I was heartbroken because neither of my daughters wanted anything to do with me. I couldn't fully blame Peaches for that. I brought all that shit on myself.

Venom had instilled so much fear in me that I was scared to breathe loudly around him. In my heart, I knew that I could have done more when he was raping Keesha, but I was also being raped and beaten everyday and she witnessed it on several occasions. I was not blaming Keesha for anything. What her father did to me was out of her control. I just wanted her to understand that I feared for both of our lives.

I was happy when she was able to escape the hell that she was living in. In her absence, I became the focus of all his rage and anger. He beat and raped me because I wasn't Peaches and that shit hurt me the most. I did everything for him and it was never enough because I wasn't that bitch. Since I was able to get away from Snake, my focus had always been to get my daughters back in my life.

I never knew what had happened to my baby Keesha. Just my fucking luck she hooked up with Peaches' long, lost twin son. God was punishing me. No matter how much I repented and asked for his forgiveness, I kept coming up short and it hurts like hell. I hated Peaches with everything inside of me and that bitch had to go. I had been watching her house for the longest waiting for her to come home, but she had been MIA.

Once I saw the newspapers, I knew why she hadn't been home in a while. That snake ass Vinny was dead. I couldn't believe after all that he had done to her and those kids; she turned around and married his ass. And people called me a stupid ass bitch. She cried everyday when her mother took her other twin from her and gave it away.

I was there for her and helped her get through it. I was there for her when her fucking kids were disowned by them fucking Italians. It was me who was there for her and comforted her. How could she just turn around and turn my fucking husband against me? Before all the bullshit, we were best friends. Two peas in a pod. Thick as thieves. When you saw one of us, you saw the other. We were inseparable. That was until we met Venom and Snake's ass.

In a matter of two years, they had turned us against each other. I never wanted to hurt her or her kids. That was all Venom. I was in no position to protest. I also was in no mood to have my ass bussed open or my ass getting beat. Now that I sat here in took in all of my ill thoughts towards Peaches, I really had no one to blame but myself. Snake was horrible to her and her kids as well. She suffered at the hands of him as well. The only difference was Thug killed his ass and capitalized off of his death.

At first, I had every intention on killing Peaches, but my kids still wouldn't have anything to do with me. I was a bitter bitch and sitting up being bitter would not make my life better. I had beautiful grandchildren that I wanted to get to know. It was not fair that Peaches got to have them all to herself and not share them. I knew that she hated me, and the feelings were mutual.

I'd learned a lot about life since I got away from Venom. I needed to not only forgive Peaches, but I also needed to stop blaming her for the way my life turned out. In order for me to get right with God, I needed to get right with Keesha and Tahari. They deserved that much.

I wanted to reach out to Keesha, but her ass was crazy just like her Daddy. When she attacked me, I saw the fire in her eyes. If Tahari didn't pull her off of me, I was sure she would have killed me with her bare hands. I was not even mad at her for attacking me anymore. I deserved that shit from not protecting her from that evil ass monster Venom.

I lost more and more respect for myself every time I thought about how he raped her repeatedly. She was just a baby. She didn't deserve the things he did to her. I was a coward and a weak ass bitch for allowing him to beat and sexually abuse her. It was one thing to treat me like shit, but I never should have allowed him to do that to her. The same went for Tahari. I never should have let him treat her the way he did either.

He never sexually abused her, but I saw the lust in his eyes. If we had held her hostage any longer, he would have raped her as well. That was another reason why I had to get her out of there.

Tahari had called me several times after the confrontation between her, Keesha, and me, but I ignored all of her calls and texts because I truly didn't know what to say to her. Now I was ready to talk with my daughters and beg for their forgiveness. If they didn't forgive me, I'd understand because I didn't deserve them anyway. I decided to send Tahari a text. I could only hope that she would respond.

I know that you don't want to have anything to do with me, but I really want to see you and your sister. All I want to do is make things right with you girls before I leave this world. Please find it in your heart to forgive me. I would love for you and Keesha to come to my home so that we can clear the air.

Chapter Twenty-Nine- Tahari
My Sister's Keeper

I read the text from Cassie over and over again. I was in a battle with my mind and my heart. My mind was telling me to run far the fuck away from Cassie. My heart was telling me to give her a chance. I wanted to run it by Keesha, but I knew she would rip me a new asshole if I even told her that I was considering going to see Cassie.

I wanted to keep the fact that she reached out to me to myself. However, I knew that if I didn't tell Thug, he would be mad at me. We're on good terms and I don't want to mess that up by keeping secrets from him, especially since I was going to go see her. I was the big sister so Keesha was going whether she wanted to or not.

I decided to go to the house that Keesha and Quaadir had been staying in. I was skeptical about going because I have never been around Quaadir without Thug being present. I was still uncomfortable around him. I admit that he didn't look at me with lust in his eyes anymore. As a matter of fact, he doesn't even say anything to me. His ass avoided me all together. Thug scared his ass straight. When I pulled up to the house, I could hear their asses arguing outside. I almost wanted to turn around and leave, but it sounded like they were straight humbugging. I rang the doorbell and banged on the door. I was getting ready to go in with my key, but the door swung open and it was Quaadir and his nose was leaking blood.

"What the hell are y'all in here doing? I could hear y'all as soon as I pulled up into the driveway."

"You better come and get this crazy bitch before I kill her?" Quaadir said as he stepped to the side and let me in. I walked around the house and found Keesha in the bathroom with a towel up to her mouth. The towel was covered in blood.

"I swear to God I'm going to kill his ass. This nigga ain't shit. I'm laying in bed next to him and he's texting some bitch he was cheating on me with back home."

Before I knew it, Keesha ran out of the bathroom and I was on her ass. She jumped over the fucking couch like she was in the Matrix. Her and Quaadir were fighting again. I swear she was an untamed animal with the way she was fucking Quaadir up. I was trying my best to break them up because they were tearing the damn house up.

"Come on now y'all stop this bullshit." As soon as I said the words, Quaadir slapped Keesha's ass so hard that she flipped over the couch. This bitch jumped up like it wasn't shit and charged his ass again. I was so damn happy when Thug, Dro, and Sarge walked through the door. They were finally able to break them apart. I was trying my best no to laugh because their asses looked like Ike and Tina when they were finished fighting in the limo.

"Calm down my nigga," Thug said as they tried to hold Quaadir back. He was trying his best to get to Keesha.

"Let that nigga go so I can fuck his ass up some more." I had to practically drag Keesha out of the front he door and make her get in the car.

"Come on, Keesha, let's go back to my house. My kitchen is finished being remodeled, we can just chill there. Plus there's something I want to talk to you about anyway." Keesha sat quietly in the passenger's seat crying her eyes out. I didn't interrupt her. I let her have a moment. I know firsthand when you're hurt, a good cry made you feel better. The entire drive was quiet. I couldn't wait to make it to the house because I definitely needed a drink after this bullshit. Keesha and Quaadir had me tired as hell tussling with their asses.

When we made it to the house, I showed Keesha where the bathroom was so that she could clean herself up. I ran straight to the kitchen. I wanted to see the job that they had done. It was beautiful; it looked like there never was a fire. Thug had all new stainless steel appliances installed. I couldn't wait to cook dinner in here. I wondered what was taking Keesha so long, so I decided to go check on her.

Before I could make it to the stairs, I had a gun to my head and a masked man was dragging Keesha down the stairs with a gun pointed at her head as well. At that moment, Thug popped up in my head. I was so busy trying to drag Keesha out of the house, I never had a chance to tell him where I was going. I watched in horror as the masked man covered Keesha's mouth with a rag. She started to fight and tussle, but whatever was on the rag knocked her out cold. Before I knew it, a rag was also placed over my mouth and everything faded to black.

****

"Wake up, you black bitch!" The sound of an unfamiliar voice made my head hurt even worse. The slaps that was delivered to my face next made me become alert real fast. Once I was able to adjust my eyes, the men still had on masks. I looked over and Keesha was on the other side of the room and masked men was standing over her. The room had white walls and no furniture in it at all. There was however a huge bay window. They had took us in broad daylight and it was now nighttime. That meant they had had us for a couple of hours.

"Who are you and what the fuck do you want from us?" Keesha yelled.

"Shut the fuck up! Who we are isn't important. How much are your husband's willing to pay to get you beautiful bitches back," the masked gunman that was standing over me said. I noticed both of the gunmen were white, so it probably was someone from the Gianelli Family.

"Stand up and strip. I want you hoes ass hole naked." I guess we weren't moving fast enough, so the gunmen let off a couple of rounds by our feet. We jumped around on the floor to keep from getting hit by one of the bullets. "I said strip. The next time I won't miss. Go grab the camcorder Dominic it's time we have a little fun before we kill these bitches."

Did this nigga just say his accomplice's name? I could tell these were two fucking amateurs. The one he called by name exited the room that we were being held in. The gunman that was still in the room with us received a phone call, so he stepped out as well.

"I can't believe we've been kidnapped by Beavis and Butthead. Did you hear him call the other one by his name? They're so stupid, they don't have us tied up or nothing. They didn't plan this out at all. This shit is comical," I said to Keesha. I looked to see what she was doing and she pulled her phone out of her back pocket.

"Look. My phone has been in my pocket all this time. They're so fucking stupid they never checked us. I just put it on silent. As long as it's on Quaadir and Thug will be able to find us. In the meantime, we have to play along and do whatever the fuck they want. Pretty soon Quaadir and Thug will realize something ain't right." I nodded my head in agreement with her. I had to get the fuck out of here and home to my husband and my babies.

Keesha was putting on a brave front, but I knew she wanted to get home to Quaadir and her girls as well. The door swung open and I was not prepared for what I saw. Ta'Jay and Barbie were being led in by the gunmen. They were naked and it looked like they had been bleeding.

"I got some company for you bitches!" They pushed Ta'Jay and Barbie so hard that Ta'Jay fell face first and on her stomach.

"Oh, my baby!" Ta'Jay hollered out in pain as she gripped her stomach. The flow of blood started to fall rapidly down her legs. We all rushed towards her, but the sound of the gunshot caused all of us to stop in our tracks.

"Get the fuck back and get naked right motherfucking now!" the gunman said as he pointed the camcorder towards us. The other gunman held two guns in his hand and had them pointed at us. Keesha and I started to undress. We all cried because Ta'Jay was in so much pain. She was laid out flat on the floor crying uncontrollably.

"Ahhhhhhhhh!" Ta'Jay let out a piercing scream. It caused all of us to look over at her. "Please help me! I think I'm in labor." We all looked at the gunmen and they were laughing and still filming us.

"All you bitches get on your knees right now!" We did as we were told. I wasn't sure what was coming next, but the one thing I knew was not about to happen neither one of these motherfuckers were about to violate my girls or me. I knew that it was out of my control, but the last thing I wanted was for my husband to see a man violating me and taking what belonged to him.

The sound of a woman's voice on the other side of the door caused both of the men to jump. They left out of the room fast as hell. I noticed that they had left the camcorder on the floor. I grabbed it and threw it up against the wall. I hoped and prayed that it broke into a million pieces.

"We have to get her out of here," Barbie said as she looked around for a way to get out of the room. At this point, Keesha and me started looking for a way out as well. I looked over and she was on the phone.

"Who are you talking to?" I asked

"Y'all have to hurry up and find us. We think Ta'Jay is in labor," Keesha was whispering into the phone.

"Oh, my God! It hurts so bad, Tahari. I want Sarge." Ta'Jay was crying so badly and she was holding onto my hand and squeezing for dear life.

"Bingo!" Barbie yelled; she had managed to unlock the lock that was holding the window closed. I jumped up and we looked out. I was so happy we were on the first floor. There was no way we were going to be able to get Ta'Jay to jump out of a window if we were on a higher level.

"Come on y'all, we have to go now before they come back. We were all naked as the day we were born, but at that moment we really didn't give a fuck. Keesha was still on the phone telling Quaadir what were attempting to do.

Barbie climbed over the railing first. Keesha and I lifted Ta'Jay over the railing and handed her to Barbie. Once we were all outside of the window, we needed to look around and found the best way to go. I knew that we were in Little Italy in. We were in a residential area that was called Garibaldi Square. The rich Italians lived over in this area. The sound of gunfire behind us caused us all to take off running, including Ta'Jay running like she wasn't in labor.

"Ahhhh!" I said as I felt excruciating pain and a burning sensation that felt like my whole upper body was on fire. I looked down and I had been hit in the shoulder. I ended up losing my balance and I fell.

"Come on, Bitch! We have to keep running." Barbie said as she yanked me up. Keesha was still on the phone with Quaadir.

"It's a park about a block from here. It's late, so I know that no one will be around. Let's go in there and wait. Tell them to come to Sheridan Park." Keesha told Quaadir what I said and she hung up. We made it to the park in no time.

We laid Ta'Jay on the bench and she was still bleeding really badly. At first, she was talking and screaming, but now she was just laying there staring up in the sky.

"Oh, my God! They need to hurry up; she's not doing good. As soon as the words left my mouth, her eyes rolled in the back of her head and she closed her eyes.

"Wake Up, Ta'Jay!" We all said as we shook her trying to get her to say something. I felt for a pulse and I felt nothing. We all started to scream and panic. That was when Thug's black Tahoe pulled up and Thug, Quaadir, Sarge, and Dro jumped out with big ass guns.

"Nooooo! Not my baby!" Sarge was screaming as he fell to his knees in front of Ta'Jay's body.

Chapter Thirty-Thug
Vengeance Is Mine

The sounds of my family crying made me shed tears. This was the saddest shit that we had ever experienced as a family. I couldn't believe that this shit was happening to us. I clenched my jaws and my balled my fist up as the beautiful Pink and fourteen Karat gold casket was lowered into the ground. The feeling of Tahari rubbing my back made me calm down just a little.

I begged her not to come to the service. The bullet did major damage to her shoulder. She should be at home resting it, but she flat out refused to stay at home. She needed to be here like the rest of the family. The sound of my sister screaming and hollering as they started to put dirt onto her baby girl's casket made me cry even more. Sarge was on his hands and knees crying as well. This shit was so sad. Little Heaven Ta'Jay was not ready for this cruel ass world.

My niece was not able to sustain the trauma from the fall and the trauma to Ta'Jay's body. Ta'Jay had actually flat lined three times and they were able to save her, but not the baby. My sister's screams and pleas had me crying like a baby. I was a Thug to my heart, but I couldn't take this shit right here. I hated to see her cry or even in pain for that matter.

"Please God! Give my baby back. I'll do anything." She was trying to stop the undertakers from lowering the casket. I had to rush over to her and pull her away. The slap she delivered to me had me shocked and speechless. She continued to hit and slap me the entire time she yelled at me

"Let me go motherfucker! This shit is all your fault. We're always getting caught up in your bullshit. My baby is dead because of you. Don't touch me! Don't you ever talk to me again! I hate you. I hate you so much. You're not my brother anymore. Stay the fuck away from me and my son. You're dead to me, Ka'Jaire. Do you hear me. You're dead."

Sarge picked her up and threw her over his shoulder. She cursed and wished death on me the entire time as he carried her out of the cemetery to the family's car. Tears streamed down my face because Ta'Jay was my world. It'd been that way since my mother brought her home from the hospital. Everything that I had done over the years had been to make sure she was straight for the rest of her life. If I could I would trade places with my niece. Part of me was dead anyway. Hearing her speak those words crushed my soul. I'd never be the same after today. I never meant to cause my sister any pain in her life. All I have ever wanted to do was protect her.

"She's just upset right now. You know she didn't mean the things that she said, "Tahari said as she tried to wrap her good arm around me. I knocked her arm away. I wasn't in the mood for that bullshit. She meant that shit and Tahari knew it. I walked away from her and went back to my car and pulled off. I had to get the fuck out of there before I spazzed the fuck out.

Once I made it the crib, I went straight to my office and opened a bottle of Remy and drunk it straight from the bottle. My phone was going off non-stop. Tahari, Peaches, and Malik would not stop calling. I got so tired of the phone ringing I threw the bitch up against the wall.

I hate you. You're dead to me. You're not my brother anymore. I kept hearing Ta'Jay saying those things to me in my head and it was driving me crazy. The more I drank the more I became numb to all the shit that was going on. It was then I made a decision that would never put my wife or my kids in jeopardy. I was done. It was over between Tahari and I. I couldn't risk hurting her or my kids anymore than I already have.

If something happened to them I wouldn't be able to handle it. If I was away from them, they would be safe. I got up and started packing my shit. Once I was satisfied with what I packed, I made my way down the stairs. As I was getting ready to walk out of the door,

Tahari and my kids walked in the door and they all wrapped their arms around me and started hugging me. At that moment, nothing else mattered in the world but them. The love I felt radiating off of their bodies onto me had me feeling really bad at the moment. Not bad enough to the point where I would change my mind and stay.

"Are you going somewhere?" Tahari looked at my luggage that was by the door.

"Go upstairs for a minute y'all let me talk to Mommy real quick. I love y'all so much."

"Love you too, Daddy," they all said in unison. I watched as Ka'Jairea carried the little babies up the stairs like the good, big sister she is. I sat down on the couch and Tahari sat beside me.

"I'm leaving. I need to get as far away from y'all as I can. I can't continue to hurt my family. I don't know what I would do if something happened to you or our kids. You have access to the money, the cars, and whatever else that I own. I just can't do this anymore."

"Ka'Jaire, I don't care about all that materialistic shit. We need you here with us. Please! I need you baby. Don't do this to me." Tahari tried to kiss on me and straddle me, but I didn't have time for that shit. I knew that if I kept talking soft she was going to find away to get me to stay. I had to take a different approach. I knew that it would hurt me to do it, but this was best for everybody.

"Get the fuck off me!" I had to push Tahari off of me forcibly. For a moment, I had forgot about her injured shoulder. I felt like shit as I watched her wince in pain. I stood up and started grabbing my suitcases.

"Please don't do this. I'm begging you." Tahari was now on her knees in front of me holding onto my legs. I'm your wife I need you. What I'm I going to tell our kids? Please don't leave me, Ka'Jaire. You promised me. Remember you promised me that you would never leave me again." I had to pull her off of the floor. She was crying so hard and that was when she started hitting me with her good arm. I opened the door and my back was facing her as I walked out.

"You broke your promise. You said you would never leave me. Why are you doing this?" I was now inside my truck and she was blocking me from driving away.

"Get the fuck out the way, Tahari!" She walked over the driver's side and she just stared at me. Tears were streaming down her eyes as she stared into mine.

"This is our ending, huh? Just like that it's over. Damn near four years of marriage. Seven beautiful kids. After everything we have been through, you're just going to leave me." Our kids were standing in the doorway. "Look at them! Look at your fucking kids, Ka'Jaire." She was grabbing my face and forcibly making me look at them because it broke my heart to look at them without tearing up. She wiped the tears from her eyes and started backing up from the truck.

"You're not a Thug. You're a fucking coward and I hate the day I met you." Tahari took her ring off and threw it at me. She walked away and never looked back. Her and the kids walked into the house and closed the door. I sat in the driveway contemplating whether or not this was what I really wanted to do. I didn't want to do it, but I had to do it.

I just prayed shit worked out for a nigga in the end. I was risking everything to keep my family safe. I pulled out of the driveway and my phone started blowing up and it was calls from Peaches and Malik. I declined all calls and I threw my phone out of the window. I needed a clear and leveled head for what I was about to do. No one knew that I had a kept the lease up on my bachelor pad. That was the place where I would take chicks to before I met Tahari. No bitch was worthy of stepping one foot into my home after what that bitch Kelis had did to me.

I was contemplating on whether or not I wanted to hit my crew up and let them know what was good. Everyone was going through so much. Malik was still healing from his wounds. Sarge was dealing with the death of his daughter and Dro was still dealing with the aftermath of what happened to him, Khia, and his Baby Momma. My niggas had enough bullshit on their plates. They had put in so much work. I think that they definitely needed a break. I knew that they would be salty at me for leaving them out of the loop, but it was for the best though.

Once I made it to my spot, I reminisced like a motherfucker. I had some good ass times in this crib. Everything was exactly the way that I had left it. Tahari would kill me if she knew I still kept this place. She had nothing to worry about though, I hadn't stepped foot in here in years. Everything in here was so outdated. It was cool though because once I handle this business in the streets, I would be letting the condo go. I had no use for it anymore.

After taking a hot shower, I laid in bed and my thoughts of Tahari invaded my mind. She went from a bad situation with the nigga Nico to a worse situation with her King Pin husband. Seeing her naked with a big ass bullet hole in her shoulder fucked me up in the head. Actually, seeing all of them naked had me feeling some type of way. They all insisted that they were never raped or touched inappropriately. That was good to know.

It still didn't make me feel any better knowing that they had been manhandled and disrespected. Once we were able to get the girls calmed down, they were able to show us where they had been held and went into details about their captors. Once they ran down the details to us, we already knew who it was that had taken them; Dominic and Vinny Gianelli. The female voice they heard had to be their mother Donatella.

After taking my shower, I got dressed and headed out to my first destination. It was two in the morning and I should have been home in bed with my wife, but instead I was dressed in black with my guns loaded and ready to blow.

For the past two weeks, I had been watching these motherfuckers coming and going without a care in the world. It must be nice, but not for long. I sat in my truck and waited for the exact time I knew these niggas would be coming home. I flamed up a fat ass Kush blunt and reflected on my future.

Despite already making the decision to become head of Thug Incorporated, the recent events that had transpired had me rethinking my entire situation. It was already a struggle running my drug empire and staying a couple of steps ahead of the law. Becoming a Mob Boss would make shit even more stressful, but make my job less harder.

I could sit back and give orders and let my crew run shit. I had nothing but faith in my niggas. I already knew that they would hold court in the streets. I was not worried about my niggas though. My concern was my family and the measures that I would need to take to ensure their safety. The stakes became greater if and when I became the Boss.

I still didn't get the chance to tell Tahari about the shit that I had inherited from my grandfather. My mind drifted back to the night when I killed his fat ass. It was the night I found Tahari beaten and bruised. That was fate like a motherfucker. I laughed to myself thinking about how I always used to tell her that it was fate that brought us together. She used to look at me like I was crazy. The tap on the window brought me out of my thoughts. My instincts made me grab my gun. I looked up and it was this nigga Quaadir dressed in all black.

"You on some solo shit, Bro." Quaadir said as he took a pull off of his cigarette. He walked around and climbed into the passenger's seat. It was odd that this nigga was even here. I distinctly told them to stop staking out the place.

"I already know what you thinking Bro. I wasn't going behind your back and doing the stakeout. I'm actually here for the same reason you are. I don't know what it is, but something inside of me told me to come here tonight. I don't know I guess you can call it twin intuition or some shit. I knew that you were here."

I was glad that he said that because I was trying my best to trust him. So, far he had proven himself not only to me, but to the rest of the family as well. I guess it was in the cards for us to meet despite the circumstances. No matter how anyone looked at it, had we not met I probably would have eventually been killed and my family would have never known why or where it came from. A black Lincoln Town car pulled into the driveway and we knew the bitch ass nigga Dominic had arrived home.

"Showtime my nigga," I said as we both tied our hoodies tight and made sure we were locked and loaded. Dominic got out of the car and started to stagger up to his door. His driver didn't even wait to make sure he got in. I didn't know what type of Italians these niggas were, but they were nothing like what the hell they showed us on TV. He was having a hard time getting in the door with his key and that made it better for us. We snuck up behind him and I hit him over the head with the gun.

"Change of plans. Let's take this nigga to the warehouse," I said as we put his ass in the truck. We were back inside of the truck getting ready to pull off when a Bentley pulled into the driveway.

We slumped down in our seats and noticed it was the bitch Donatella and her other son Vinny Jr.

"We should grab both of their asses right now, we might not ever get the chance again," Quaadir said as he glanced back to make sure Dominic was still out cold.

"We can kill that bitch here. I want that nigga Vinny chained up in my warehouse."

"This nigga out cold. Let's go in kill the bitch and grab our long, lost brother." We both laughed and checked Dominic one last time before we exited the car again. We crept back up to the door and it was slightly open. We rushed in without hesitation. Vinny was standing at the bar with his back turned and before he could get a word out, I started pistol whooping his ass with no mercy. All I saw was the girls naked and my nieces casket being lowered into the ground. At first he was squirming, but eventually, his body went limp and I let his body fall to the floor.

"What the hell is all that noise you're making?" Donatella said as she came back towards the foyer where we were standing. "Noooo!" she screamed at the same Quaadir shot her right between the eyes. She fell face first and the blood started to pour profusely.

"Your ass a sharp shooter or something," I had to ask him. He hit her ass with so much precision that it was like something out of a movie.

"I was raised by Aunt Ruth, one of the best gun slingers the A has ever seen. She taught me everything I know." Quaadir picked

Vinny Jr. up off the floor and threw him over his shoulder. We were in and out in a matter of minutes and in route to the warehouse.

At first, I wanted to keep my niggas out of loop. However, Sarge deserved to be here to get some get back for his daughter and his wife. I had to really think about the shit. If it was me in his shoes, I would definitely want in on killing the niggas who harmed my wife and caused my daughter's death. I wanted to inform Malik, but he was in no condition to be out torturing niggas. I'd make sure to get them niggas on behalf of him for hurting my sister-in-law.

Chapter Thirty-One- Ta'Jay
Worst Feeling Ever

I hadn't been able to eat or sleep since I lost my daughter. Barbie and I had just left the doctor's office when we were snatched from the parking lot. When we were on our way there, Barbie kept saying that she felt like we were being followed. I told her that she was just being paranoid. I should have listened to her when she said that we should call somebody because I refused and now I was regretting it. I hadn't been out of my room since my daughter's funeral service.

I kept staring at the professional pictures I had taken of her before they took her down to the morgue. She was dressed in a beautiful white dress with a huge bow on her head. She was so cute with a head full of hair. She was the splitting image of her father. Sarge and I took pictures with her and we made sure to get her some by herself. Most people wouldn't do that, but I wanted something to remember her by. I would never get to see her take her first steps or speak her first words. That hurt me so much.

My baby girl didn't deserve to die at the hands of people who were out for my brother or anybody else for that matter. My phone had been ringing non-stop and I didn't want to talk to anybody. I was glad my mother had my son. I was in no condition to look after him right now. My bedroom door opened and Sarge walked in. I turned my back to his ass. I had no words for him either. I was just about fed up with him and his street life. He was a part of my brother's team, so he was guilty by association.

"You really need to get your ass out of this bed and go get our son," Sarge said as he walked inside our bedroom closet and started changing clothes.

"I don't have to do shit. Leave me the fuck alone and let me mourn our daughter. Unlike you who seems not to give a fuck that she's dead."

"Don't ever let no shit like that fly out your mouth again. You of all people know how fucked up I am about Heaven. I can't believe you would even say some shit like that to me. Then again I'm not surprised at anything that comes out of your smart ass mouth." Sarge sat on the side of the bed and started lacing up his boots.

"What the fuck is that supposed to mean?" I was now sitting up in bed and staring his ass down.

"It means exactly how it sounds. I'm not about to sugarcoat shit with your ass. The way you behaved at the cemetery was uncalled for. That shit you said to your brother was real fucked up. He goes so hard for you. Do you have any idea how fucked up he is behind you saying the shit you said to said to him?"

"This is not about Ka'Jaire right now. This is about me and the fact that my daughter is dead. What about me, Sarge? Does anybody care about me and what I'm going through?" I jumped up from the bed and got all the way up in his face. I couldn't believe Sarge was acting as if my feelings didn't matter and he was really pissing me off.

"Is all about you huh, Ta'Jay? Fuck the fact that the entire family is going through shit because the world revolves around Ta'Jay. Your ass ain't nothing but a spoiled bitch!" He put emphasis on the world bitch and it made me jump back. We've argued before, but he had never disrespected me this way.

"How dare you disrespect me?" My emotions got the best of me and I hauled off and slapped him across the face.

"Have you lost your fucking mind? Don't you ever put your fucking hands on me." Sarge had his hands wrapped around my throat and choking me with so much force that I started to see spots in my eyes. I was clawing and hitting his chest to get him to stop. I guess something snapped inside of him and just let me go. I fell to the floor and started to grasp for air.

"Oh, my God! You tried to kill me."

"I didn't try to kill your ass. I just wanted to give you a motherfucking reality check. You're not fucking with no lame ass nigga. Think twice before you put your fucking hands on me." Sarge walked out of the room and left out of the house. I just laid on the floor and I cried. I knew that I was spoiled rotten. I just never knew that my actions had the potential to affect my family. The words that Sarge said to me had me thinking about Thug. How could I say those things to him? He had been the best brother in the world. Most girls dreamt of having a big brother like Thug. Here I was I had him in my life and I treated him like dirt underneath my shoes. I loved my brother and I was just mad. I never meant to hurt him. I was wrong for blaming him for my daughter's death. He would've fought tooth and nail to save my baby.

"Oh, my God! How could I say that shit to him?" I screamed out loud. I'm sure my neighbors and everyone else in our Cul-de-sac could hear me. I needed to get to my brother's house and apologize to him for everything I said to him. I got up and threw on anything I could find. I didn't care that it was five in the morning. I needed to get to my brother and apologize. I called his phone over and over again. It just kept rolling over to voicemail.

****

"Open the door, Ka'Jaire. I know that you're in there. I need to talk to you!" I had been banging on the door and leaning on the doorbell. It took damn near forty-five minutes to get to their crib. The sun was coming up, so I knew that someone was woke in the house. The twins wake up at the crack of dawn when I kept them. so I knew for a fact somebody was woke.

"I'm sorry for everything I said to you, Ka'Jaire! Just please open the door and talk to me." I was about to give up until I heard the locks being undone. Tahari was standing there looking sad as ever.

"Where is Thug? I need to apologize to him for the things I said." I tried to step inside of the house, but she stepped in my way blocking me from entering.

"He's not here and I don't know where he's at. The shit you said to him sent him off the deep end. He packed his shit and left because he doesn't want anyone else in the family to get hurt."

"Oh, my God! What have I done, Tahari? How could I be so cruel? He's done nothing but love and protect me since I was a baby."

"The things you said to him hurt him so bad. I have never seen him look so defeated. I'm sorry I don't know where he is. Honestly, I really don't give a fuck. He made it perfectly clear that he was leaving me and my children. If you don't mind, I need to cook breakfast for my babies." Tahari tried to close the door in my face like I was nothing.

"Are you serious right now? How could you say that you don't give a fuck?" I had my foot in the door blocking her from closing it.

"I meant just what I said. I don't give a fuck. Obviously, Thug needs his space to find himself. I'm not about to stress myself out anymore than I already have, If it's meant for us to be together, he will do what he needs to do and find his way home to his family. In the meantime, I have seven fucking kids to raise. Since you're the reason why he left, how about you go look for him because I'm not." Tahari slammed the door in my face and I stood there in shock. She made me feel even worse. My words really fucked him up in the head. He would never leave Tahari or his kids. I drove back to my house in tears. I cried for Heaven, I cried for Thug, and I cried for my marriage.

Heaven was gone and that hurt so bad. The things I said to Thug not only hurt him, but caused him to bring pain to the people he loved the most. The words Sarge said to me replayed over and over in my head. I had to really be a spoiled bitch for Sarge to say it to me. He was so angry when he left. I had already lost Heaven. I was sure Thug would never look at me the same again. I needed Sarge. I couldn't bear losing him, too.

Chapter Thirty-Two-Sarge
Payback is a Bitch

The fact that Ta'Jay could be so selfish hearted had me rethinking our whole relationship. Losing my daughter hurt like hell. I cried until my eyes hurt when the doctor came out and told me she didn't make it. I wanted to turn around and go back and choke her ass again for saying the foul ass shit that she said to me. I had no words for her after the performance she put on at the cemetery.

The shit she said to her brother was way out of line. Before I even looked at her in a sexual way, I noticed how Malik, Thug, and Peaches spoiled her rotten. Anything she asked for she got it. I didn't make it any better because when I came into her life, I started spoiling her even more than they did. She was now my wife and my responsibility. I could buy her a black Birken bag today and tomorrow she would come back and say she wanted in white. I would go out and get it with no questions asked. Mainly, because I didn't want her walking around pouting and acting like it was the end of the fucking world.

I couldn't even be mad at her though that was the way that she was before I married her. Thug, Malik, and Peaches had created a monster. Besides all that, Thug still didn't deserve for her to be so disrespectful to him. I hated to put my hands on her like that. I'd never done anything like that even when she had hit me first in the past. I would just walk away. That was what I should have done, but she chose the wrong day to go far with me.

As soon as I get back home, I was going to apologize to her. I loved her spoiled ass she just made me want to kick her ass sometimes. I was happy as hell when Thug called and told me to come to the warehouse. That could only mean one thing; he had a package for me, and it needed to be unwrapped.

"It took your ass long enough," Thug said out of breathe as him and Quaadir continued to beat the fuck out who I believed to be Dominic and Vinny Jr. It was kind of fucked up because here it was brothers against brothers. I didn't feel sorry for their asses though. It was their fucking fault my daughter was six feet under.

"I got into it with your crazy ass sister." As soon as I said that, Thug started to hit Dominic's ass even harder.

"Just kill me you black motherfuckers!" Vinny said as he spit blood out onto the floor.

"I got you homie. Don't worry about it," I said as I kicked both of their asses out of the chair. I walked over and grabbed a Hazmat suit and goggles; this shit was about to get real messy. Thug knew what was up so he suited up as well. Quaadir stood there looking at us like he was crazy.

"If you don't want these fuck boi's blood on you. I suggest you suit up." The sound of us cranking up the Chainsaws caused Dominic and Vinny to squirm like the cowards that they were. Piece by piece we cut their bodies parts up and placed them into plastic bags and then inside huge storage containers. We called the cleanup crew to handle the mess inside the warehouse. Thug, Quaadir, and I wanted to personally deliver the body parts to Don Gianelli. We pulled up to the estate and threw the containers into the driveway. The security guard never seen or heard anything; he was too busy sleeping.

It was ten in the morning when I finally made it back to the crib. I came in and went straight upstairs to take a shower. I bagged the clothes and shoes I had on and got rid of everything. Ta'Jay wasn't at home. A part of me wondered where she could be. The other part really didn't give a fuck. Mainly, because I knew she was somewhere in her feelings and sulking. I hadn't had much sleep since the day she was kidnapped and my daughter died.

I was dead ass tired and all I wanted to do was sleep. My intentions were to only take a short nap. I ended up sleeping until nine o'clock at night. I rolled over in bed and noticed that Ta'Jay's side of the bed was empty. I got out of bed and went to see if I could find her. As I walked down the hallway, I heard sniffles coming from the nursery we had prepared for Heaven. I took a deep breath before I entered the room. Ta'Jay was sitting on the floor holding the pictures of our daughter. I sat down on the floor next to her.

"She was beautiful like you," I said to her as I grabbed her hand in mine.

"No, Heaven was the splitting image of you and Sar'Jay." She wiped her eyes and laid her head on my shoulder. "Why did she have to die, Sarge? She was so innocent."

"I know that you're upset right now, but we can't question God. He had bigger plans for her that required her presence. That's why I named her Heaven. We're going to get through this together."

"I'm sorry for slapping you. You didn't deserve that." Ta'Jay held my face in her hands.

"No, I'm the sorry one. I never should have chocked you." We kissed and hugged each other tightly.

"Do you think my brother will forgive me for all the awful things I said to him?"

"Of course he will. Just give him some time to get his head together. He has a lot on his plate right now. He loves your spoiled ass. Always has and always will."

"I hope so. Come on let's go to bed. I haven't felt you inside of me in so long. I need some of that Daddy Dick to make me feel better." For the rest of the night, we made love to each other and discussed trying to have another baby in the future. Having another baby would never replace our baby girl Heaven. She would always be our first daughter and our guardian angel.

Chapter Thirty-Three-Thug
I'm A Outlaw Got A Outlaw Chick

It had been a week since I walked out on my wife and kids. I felt like shit for not calling or sending a text. I could hear her now calling me everything but the child of God. No matter what, I knew that she was holding down the home front. I still hadn't got a new phone, so no one was able to get in touch with me. I decided not to get a phone because I would be tempted to pick up it up and call and my wife. The last part of my plan was not completed just yet. I needed to tie up one last loose end. This fat motherfucker Don Gianelli was still alive and ticking, but not for long. It had been a couple of days since the triple funeral of his daughter and grandsons. The news report said that it was a Mob hit stemming from an ongoing Mob war.

I had been following Don Gianelli for a whole week. He stayed with four or more bodyguards everywhere he went. Except one place--The Pink Monkey strip club. He always made them stay outside. On this day in particular, I decided to go inside just to see if I could get close to him. This strip club was upscale so there was already security throughout the facility. I observed Don Gianelli sit at the foot of the stage. I ordered a drink and sat in one of the booths. I couldn't risk being seen by his ass.

I had my fitted cap pulled down low over my eyes as I watched him get a lap dance by one of the baddest bitches in the room. She was dressed in a hot a pink two piece panty and bra set and a mask to match it. The hot pink lipstick on her lips complimented her beautiful skin. It looked like he was about to bust a nut right there. The stripper whispered something in his ear and he pushed away the rest of the strippers.

She grabbed his hand and led him to the back where they did private dances. He was happier than a kid in a candy store. I looked around to see if I saw a security guard paying attention. It was just my luck that was all preoccupied with breaking up a fight. I quickly made my way to the back. I pulled my gun from my waist and screwed on the silencer. I checked two rooms before I came to the third room. I peeked inside the curtain and I noticed Don Gianelli ass hole naked staring down the barrel of a pearl handled nine-millimeter. The stripper was getting ready to off his ass.

"If it's money you want you can have everything in my pockets. Just please don't kill me," he was begging and pleading for his life.

"This ain't about money motherfucker. It's about respect. You disrespected my Clyde and that makes Bonnie very unhappy."

"Do you have any motherfucking idea who I am you black bitch!"

"Who you are isn't important. However, you should have did your homework on who the fuck I am! My husband Thug sends his love." She raised the gun emptied the entire clip in his ass. I hid in one of the empty rooms as I peeked out and watched Tahari flee the scene out of the emergency exit. I made sure the coast was clear and got my ass the fuck out of dodge. I went back to the condo that I was staying in and tried to take in what I had just seen.

Tahari had taken out the head nigga. I didn't know if I should be mad or proud as hell. I packed my shit fast as hell; I needed to get home to my wife. I needed to know how the fuck Ta-Baby managed to pull this shit off without anybody knowing it. Her ass was slicker than a can of oil. I must admit it though she looked sexy than a motherfucker offing that nigga. As I jumped in my truck, I had to adjust my dick. Picturing Ta-Baby in that hot pink suit had me horny as hell.

****

I'm an Outlaw got a Outlaw chick

Bumping 2PAC

On my outlaw shit

Jay Z and Beyonce's hit song *On The Run* was blasting through the speakers of our surround sound system. The smell of my favorite chicken and shrimp Alfredo permeated the air. I walked into the kitchen and Tahari was standing over the stove cooking in one of my tanks, a pair of red lace booty shorts, and cheetah print Red Bottoms. I was turned on but confused as hell at the moment.

"What's up baby?" I said getting her attention.

"Hey Bae. I missed you so much." She walked over and wrapped her arms around my neck and kissed me on the lips. "Sit down so you can eat. I cooked your favorite." I sat down and I immediately started to eat. I hadn't had a decent meal in over two weeks. Tahari sat at the table with me, but she didn't eat. She sat and sipped on her wine.

"You're not going to eat anything?"

"No. It's all about you tonight. Hurry up and eat. Your bathwater is getting cold." I prayed she wasn't about to fuck me up next for leaving her and the kids. For the moment, I would just go with the flow. After I was finished eating, Tahari led me upstairs and undressed me from head to toe and led me to our bathroom. I sat inside the hot tub of water.

Tahari handed me a lit blunt and a glass of Remy. She took my AXE body wash and started to clean my entire blunt. She had a nigga feeling like a fucking King. For a brief moment, my mind drifted away from the fact that my wife had just killed the Don of one of the biggest Mafia families. I knocked backed the glass of Remy and poured myself another shot.

"Let me ask you something. Why are you pampering me? I should be the one pampering you." I took a pull from the blunt and exhaled the smoke in to the air. I leaned my head back because

Tahari was now washing the family jewels. Tahari knew exactly what she was doing to me.

"You deserve to be pampered. I know that you've been stressed out. I just want to make you feel better." She gestured for me to get out of the tub and she dried me off. Tahari led me to the bed and she began to rub massage oil all over me

"I just want to let you know that I know why you left and I'm not mad. At first, I didn't understand. That was until I sat back and put two and two together. You would never leave us like that unless you had a good reason You did what you had to do to protect us and I love you for that. You're the best husband and father in the world."

"How did you manage to get to Don Gianelli before me?"

"That shit was easy. You led me to him. Did you forget that you had put GPS tracking systems on all of our cars? I've been following you for the last week. At first, I wasn't going to come after you. I knew I had to let you do you, but that shit didn't sit too well with me. The ride or die bitch in me couldn't sit at home and let you hold court in the streets without me."

"I don't even know what to say, Ma. You stay holding a nigga down no matter what." I pulled her close to me and hugged her tight around the waist.

"Don't say anything. Come on let's make love. We have a Mob Legacy to build."

"You know about that too, huh?"

"I'm your wife, your best friend, the mother of your children, and your Bonnie. It's my job to know everything about you." Tahari pulled her tank over her head and pulled off her panties.

"Leave them shoes on I want to make love to you while you're wearing them. Lay down and let me look at my pretty pink pussy." Tahari laid back and I admired the work of art in front of me. She had them raised so far back they were almost behind her head, giving me all access to what belonged to me. I took the glass of Remy I had and poured it on her pussy. I licked and slurped it all up. Tahari had a nigga drunk in love as her pussy juices and the Remy marinated on my tongue. I positioned myself in between her legs and slid into her love box. Her pussy muscles grabbed my dick and held it hostage as I slowly slid in and out of her.

"Oh, shit, Ka'Jaire!" I knew I wasn't hitting it right if she was calling me by my government. Without warning, I flipped her over and rammed my dick inside of her. I smacked her on the ass repeatedly as I sped up the pace as I began to fuck her brains out.

"What's my motherfucking name!"

"Oh, my God!" she screamed out in pleasure.

"Wrong answer. I said what's my motherfucking name!" I roughly grabbed her hair and I smacked her ass as hard as I could.

"Thuuggggg!!" She gripped the sheets as she screamed out in pain and pleasure. "Please, baby don't stop giving me this Thug Passion. I'm about to cum."

"Well, come then. Let all that shit out." Tahari creamed all over my dick and collapsed on the bed breathing heavily. I laid down beside her and she laid her head on my chest.

"You love it when I give you that Thug Passion."

"Yes. I've loved that shit ever since the first time we made love. I'm going to love that shit forever." She placed soft kisses all over my body and for the rest of the night we made love like nothing or nobody else existed in the world.

Epilogue

1 Year Later

The sound of Thug's Salvatore Ferragamo's and Tahari's Red Bottoms clicking across the marble floor caused everyone in the room to come to a complete silence. As usual their powerful demeanor commanded attention wherever they went. Nothing was different today. Some of the most powerful and ruthless Mob Bosses from around the world sat at the roundtable. They were in awe that such a young black man and woman was respected and feared at the same time.

It was the monthly meeting where all of the Heads of the family would come together and discuss business over drinks and good food. Thug and Tahari never ate or drank anything. They would just sit back, observe, and take notes. Tahari was the only woman at these meetings. Traditionally, a woman would never be able to sit at the roundtable, but most women weren't Tahari Kenneth. Thug knew that the men hid their hard ons as his wife walked into the room with her designer dresses on and draped in her diamonds. She was the wife of a Boss and Thug made sure she looked the part each and every time they walked out of the door. No one even called her Tahari anymore. She was simply, "Boss Lady".

Once Thug took his rightful place as a Mob Boss; he vowed that he would never run his family the traditional Mafia way. He would run it just like he always had. Only this time, everyone would have titles beside their names. Thug went by his own rules and did whatever the fuck he wanted and there was nothing anyone could do about it.

Once Thug took control of the Santerelli Family, he also took power and territory from the Gianelli Family. Both families were the only Mob factions operating in Chicago. Now that Thug reigned supreme over everything, he was now one of the most powerful Mob Bosses the Mafia had ever seen. He was already the King of the Chi, but now he owned the whole city out right.

Thug Inc. consisted of only family and a few of his most loyal men. He didn't feel the need to have a bunch of niggas on his team who never put their lives on the line with him. He refused to break bread with niggas who could be the cause of his downfall or his death. He worked too hard to get where he was.

Malik and Quaadir were the Under Bosses. Dro and Sarge were Enforcers and Thug had gave them control of their own territory. Over the years, they had put in so much work. They deserved to have free reign and make money that went straight to them. King had proved himself to Thug and he now sat in Thug's old position. Nasir and Dutch worked underneath them. The three young men had come a long way from being the local jack boys. Once they met Thug, he offered them a better way of getting money. It had been on and popping ever since.

****

Once the meeting was over, Tahari and Thug made their way back to the Kenneth Estate. Don Santerelli had left so much land to Thug that he was able to build Tahari her dream home from the ground up. The house was built off the beaten path. Only family would be able to find out where it was. This time around Thug took the extra steps to ensure that his family was safe and away from their old lives. He knew for a fact his new status was sure to bring new enemies. The last thing he wanted was for his family to be hurt again.

Thug pulled into the winding driveway and wondered why the rest of the family was at his home. He hoped and prayed that nothing bad at happened. He hadn't received a phone call so he knew it couldn't be that. He looked over at Tahari and she wasn't concerned about it. That meant she already knew what was up. They exited the car and made their way into the house. Once they finally stepped into the foyer of their beautiful home, everyone stood to their feet and started to clap for him. He was trying to figure out what all this was for, so he looked over at Tahari for some type of clue.

"All of this is for you baby. Everyone just wanted to come and show you how much they appreciate all you do for this family." Tahari kissed Thug on the lips and slipped him some tongue. Malik, Quaadir, Dro, Sarge, King, Nasir, and Dutch all embraced their brother and Boss and dapped him up. Markese, Rahmeek, Kills, and Boogie did the same and handed him a briefcase that contained one million dollars. Thug insisted that they take the briefcase back. They were family. However, Markese insisted that he take it.

Thug was now head of the family and as long as his pockets were fat the rest of the families would be fat as well. Markese told Thug it was out of respect. Family had nothing to do with it. Ta'Jay, Barbie, Khia, and Keesha all embraced Thug and kissed him on the jaw. Trish, Aja, Stacy, Nisa, and Gail all did the same. Gail held her embrace just a little longer. She made sure to let him know that she was so proud of him. His favorite girl in the world Peaches hugged her son and kissed him all over his face. He had to pry her off of him and that made everybody laugh. Of course Peaches didn't find anything funny and went on a cursing spree.

After eating the dinner that had been professionally prepared, everyone sat around and just enjoyed each other's company. For the first time in a long time, everyone was together for a joyous and happy occasion. Not because it was beef in the streets and their lives were in danger. He couldn't help but smile as he looked at everyone in the room.

He was thankful that Ta'Jay really didn't blame him for Heaven's death. That lifted a large weight off of his shoulders. Ta'Jay and Sarge looked like they were the happiest they had been in a long time. She had recently given birth to another son Sema'Jay. Thug laughed a little as he looked at Barbie talking shit as usual; loud as ever. It seemed like Lil Malik coming into their lives made them stronger. Diamond had succumbed to Breast Cancer two months after she dropped him off. Barbie recently gave birth to another baby girl she named Paris. Malik had healed from his gunshot wounds and was looking like brand new money.

Thug shook his head as he looked over at Keesha and Quaadir arguing. All they did was fight and argue, but the love they had was evident. It warmed Thug's heart to see Keesha and Tahari become some close; after all they shared the same mother and the same ruthless father. After never getting a response from Tahari about forgiving her, Cassie killed herself. She left everything she owned to Keesha, Tahari, and to all of her grandchildren. She even left something for Ka'Jaire Jr. and Ka'Jairea. That made Thug have a little more respect for her.

Thug thought about how crazy it was that at one point they had been gunning for one another, now they were inseparable. Peaches called him, Malik, and Quaadir the Three Musketeers. Quaadir turned everything over to one of his associates in Atlanta. He made it up in his mind that he would never be separated from his family again.

Khia and Dro's relationship was better than ever. Khia had legally adopted Dro's kids. They had finally come around and fell in love with her. Peaches was sipping Patron and smoking on her cigarettes as usual. Vinny's money looked damn good on her. He left her a gold mine and she was taking full advantage of it. Thug knew that spending the money and taking lavish trips was her way of hiding her hurt and anger, not to mention the little boy toy she had been messing with. Peaches had turned into a Cougar. He didn't like the shit one bit.

Thug felt a since of pride as Ka'Jaire Jr., Ka'Jairea, Kaine, Kash, Ka'Jaiyah, Kaia, and Ka'hari came downstairs to hug and kiss him and Tahari before Marta put them in the bed for the night. All that he had worked so hard for would not be a vain. One day his sons and daughters would run his empire and carry on his Legacy.

Last but not least, he smiled and adjusted his hard on as he watched Tahari work the room. The way her ass and breasts looked in her bondage dress made him want to put everybody out and make love to her right then and there. He was patient though because he knew at the end of the night, he would have her in every position imaginable. Tahari caught Thug staring at her ass, so she walked over to him and whispered in his ear.

"You like something you see, Boss."

"I like everything I see, Boss Lady," he said as he hit her on the ass.

"Let's go upstairs. I've been feenin for some of that Thug Passion." Tahari reached down and grabbed his manhood. He stood up and grabbed her hand and led her upstairs to their bedroom. It didn't matter that they had a house full of people. Fulfilling each other's needs was more important. As he laid her down and undressed her, his mind was flooded with visions of the past.

When the odds were stacked against them and it didn't look like they would make it, but here they were after all the bullshit still going strong. He would no longer be giving her Thug Passion that was a thing of the past. It was a new day and new era. He would now be giving her Thug Paradise.

THE END

COMING SOON

THUG PARADISE: A NEW CHAPTER

CPSIA information can be obtained
at www.ICGtesting.com
Printed in the USA
LVOW04s1747021216

515533LV00010B/878/P